A Billion-Dollar Family

A bond worth billions!

After graduating Harvard as best mates, Trace Jackson, Wyatt White and Cade Smith formed the billion-dollar company that made them all superrich. Now life has forced them to go in different directions, but they're still as close as can be.

But while they were successful in business, these tycoons haven't been successful in love...until now... Because they're about to meet the women who will change their lives, and their ideas about family, forever!

Trace heads to Tuscany with the aim of forgetting his past and finds so much more in:

Tuscan Summer with the Billionaire

Available now!

And look for Wyatt's and Cade's stories, coming soon!

Dear Reader,

Have you ever wondered what it would be like if you unexpectedly received an offer for the business that had been your life's work? The money is too good to turn down, but suddenly you're unemployed. The business that kept you busy and happy is now gone and you're alone with your thoughts.

That's what happened to Trace Jackson. Rather than torment himself thinking about his past, he buys a vineyard so he can be the happy vintner, greeting tourists, showing everyone a good time. But he hadn't planned on the Giordano Vineyards' general manager, Marcia Giordano, being so beautiful or so tempting. Still, he's got secrets that preclude him from moving on.

Marcia, on the other hand, has a past that's been blasted all over town. Everyone knows her ex-fiancé embezzled from the vineyard and walked away, pushing her family to the brink of bankruptcy. She has trust issues, but more than that, the humiliation has beaten her down.

Trace decides to help her get beyond her mistakes, putting his heart at risk...but in the end, could it be that Marcia saves him?

I hope you enjoy Marcia and Trace's story as much as I did.

Susan Meier

Tuscan Summer with the Billionaire

Susan Meier

Recycling programs
for this product may
not exist in your area.

ISBN-13: 978-1-335-56700-0

Tuscan Summer with the Billionaire

Copyright © 2021 by Linda Susan Meier

All rights reserved. No part of this book may be used or reproduced in
any manner whatsoever without written permission except in the case of
brief quotations embodied in critical articles and reviews.

This is a work of fiction. Names, characters, places and incidents
are either the product of the author's imagination or are used fictitiously.
Any resemblance to actual persons, living or dead, businesses,
companies, events or locales is entirely coincidental.

This edition published by arrangement with Harlequin Books S.A.

For questions and comments about the quality of this book,
please contact us at CustomerService@Harlequin.com.

Harlequin Enterprises ULC
22 Adelaide St. West, 40th Floor
Toronto, Ontario M5H 4E3, Canada
www.Harlequin.com

Printed in U.S.A.

Susan Meier is the author of over fifty books for Harlequin. *The Tycoon's Secret Daughter* was a Romance Writers of America RITA® Award finalist, and *Nanny for the Millionaire's Twins* won the Book Buyers Best Award and was a finalist in the National Readers' Choice Awards. Susan is married and has three children. One of eleven children herself, she loves to write about the complexity of families and totally believes in the power of love.

Books by Susan Meier

Harlequin Romance

Christmas at the Harrington Park Hotel

Stolen Kiss with Her Billionaire Boss

The Missing Manhattan Heirs

Cinderella's Billion-Dollar Christmas
The Bodyguard and the Heiress
Hired by the Unexpected Billionaire

Manhattan Babies

Carrying the Billionaire's Baby
A Diamond for the Single Mom
Falling for the Pregnant Heiress

The Princes of Xaviera

Pregnant with a Royal Baby!
Wedded for His Royal Duty

A Mistletoe Kiss with the Boss
The Boss's Fake Fiancée
The Spanish Millionaire's Runaway Bride

Visit the Author Profile page
at Harlequin.com for more titles.

For the real Marcia, my bowling bud, who wanted her own book. The name is the same, though the life circumstances are a tad different since she doesn't live in a villa in Tuscany.
Kisses, Friend Marcia!

Praise for
Susan Meier

CHAPTER ONE

TRACE JACKSON SLOWED his red Maserati and made the turn at the sign announcing Giordano Vineyards, the property for which he'd assumed ownership that morning. He kept his speed low as he took in the grounds, awestruck by the long rows of grapes, the hills and valleys covered in green grass and trees, and the blue, blue sky.

He was now Trace Jackson, Tuscan vintner. Soon he would be the guy who laughed with tourists at wine-tasting events and the guy who relaxed on the back patio of his villa as evening descended. Holding a glass of red, he would gaze at his beautiful property, not haunted by the past or pushed toward the future, just being himself.

Nothing else.

No more ghosts. No more memories.

The three-story ivory stucco house with dark brown shutters came into view. The vineyard was closed to guests that day while it left the hands of the Giordano family and passed into his. The entire property shimmered with stillness.

He finished the drive down the lane and got out of his car. Taking a long, satisfied breath, he admired the new winemaking facility complete with gift shop and two tasting bars, then the manicured lawn and the multicar garage.

A warm June breeze ruffled his short hair, as he retrieved his bag from the trunk, then half jogged to the villa door. But he stopped and took one more look around the grounds, unable to believe this place was his, that he was about to become a vintner, that he was starting a whole new life. Then he pressed in the numbers for the lock and pushed on the thick wood door.

Glancing around the echoing foyer, he set his bag on a bench in front of the stairway that curled to the second-floor hall. Three tall windows gracefully ascended the wall beside it. The sconce lights between the windows added elegance to the polished space with marble floors and dark-stained steps that complemented the embellished black wrought-iron railing.

A sound in the back had his head jerking to the left. Knowing the house was supposed to be empty, he walked through the bare living room and the almost bare dining room—which still had the long table and chairs that had been negotiated in the sale—toward the great room, where he stopped.

A short, shapely woman stood in front of the wall of windows, staring out at the rows of grapes on a hillside just beyond the manicured lawn. Her hunched shoulders and the way her hands gripped her elbows as if she were hugging herself spoke of sadness or maybe defeat. The room suddenly filled with it. All the joy he'd experienced as he'd gotten out of his car and entered his new home evaporated. Cast away by her sorrow.

Not happy with that or the intruder, he said, "Excuse me?"

His voice echoed around him in the hollow, high-ceilinged room.

The woman slowly turned. Long black corkscrew curls framed a face with delicate features that looked to have been fashioned by the gods. A lightweight pink sweater outlined the kind of curves a man itched to get his fingers on.

His heart jolted and he almost laughed at himself. After his divorce, he'd vowed never to marry again, so he only dated tall, leggy redheads. Women who looked nothing like his blonde ex-wife. He'd never given much thought to brunettes. But this brunette was stunning.

"Signor Jackson?"

When she said his name, he realized she was probably an employee of the vineyard there to greet him, and he extended his hand to her.

"Yes. But you can call me Trace."

She shook his hand. "I'm Marcia. General manager."

"Oh!" He took a second to process that. He

wasn't sure why he'd thought the general manager was a man. But…whatever. They'd had plenty of female executives at the holding company he and his partners had owned until a few months ago. He had no bias. He could work with anybody.

"It's a pleasure to meet you. Thank you for agreeing to stay on and teach me the ropes."

She snorted. "I did not agree."

"But the sales contract—"

Her brown eyes flashed. "My father doesn't ask permission. He also didn't bother to ask forgiveness when I told him I wasn't chattel he could barter in a business deal. He simply told me he'd put it in the clause, and I had to abide by it."

"It's part of the transition. Lots of companies have employees stay behind to help the new owner. Besides, you're not the only one in the agreement. Your brothers are staying too."

"*Si*, they'll stay for a few months. I'll stay a year."

"You're the general manager. Your job's a little more complex than running the wine-tasting room."

She snorted. "You think you're going to pick up how to handle customers in a few weeks?" She shook her head. "It's not as easy as it sounds."

"Doesn't matter. They'll be here tomorrow morning to start showing me their jobs. What I pick up I pick up. What I don't I'll figure out when the time comes."

She shook her head and paced the room. Her body moved fluidly, with a grace and elegance that mesmerized him.

He caught himself, confused by the direction of his thoughts, but more baffled by her. It didn't seem right that someone so angry could make a man's mind go blank from attraction. Especially his. He was all business, no nonsense. He didn't even tiptoe over the line into personal feelings or issues when it came to work.

He blamed his lapse on time zones and hormones. And all that glorious hair. It had been a while since a woman's looks had entranced him. He'd reacted because he hadn't been prepared for it.

No big deal.

She gestured back the way he'd come. "My duties today include showing you around." She gave him a quick once-over and he'd never felt more deficient. "Whether I want to or not."

Okay. So, his general manager's problem went a little deeper than job dissatisfaction. Were he to hazard a guess, he'd say she was more than unhappy to be stuck with *him* for the year her father had promised she would stay at the vineyard.

He headed for the door, thinking through options. He could fire her and hire someone else who knew as much as she did. In this part of Italy, vineyards were everywhere. Surely, he could find a replacement. Or he could feel her out. See just how angry she was and if that anger would spill over into their work. Lots of angry people were competent. Keeping her would be easier than replacing her, but he'd replaced indispensable people before. Because that's what he did. That's why he was successful. He could adapt.

Another situation flitted through his brain. He'd thought he'd adapted to that, but now he wasn't so sure. Still, that was why he was here. In quiet Tuscany. Starting over.

With the right questions, he could probably have Marcia Giordano figured out in ten minutes.

Marcia let Trace Jackson lead the way to the front door and she stifled a groan. The view from the back was even better than the front. Shiny black hair and blue eyes the color of a perfect sky had almost had her forgetting how furious she was with her dad for selling the vineyard. Add tortoiseshell glasses that made him look like a smart, savvy businessman, as well as a gray suit, white shirt and wine-colored tie, and, sure, she might have had the urge to fan herself. Now, she could see his broad shoulders, tapered waist and what appeared to be a very tight butt.

She tamped down the surge of feminine curiosity. This was no time to be soft. This was war. She needed to get this vineyard back into her family's hands to make up for the fact that it was her fiancé, Adam, who had embezzled the money the Giordano family had borrowed to build the new wine facility, forcing her father to borrow more money and getting them so far into debt he had to sell.

That was why *she* had to buy it back.

Not her dad. Not her brothers. *She* had to fix this.

Trace Jackson opened the door and motioned for her to exit first. Politely. Gallantly.

She held back a sigh. She didn't want him to be nice. That would just make this more difficult. "We don't go overboard with courtesies here."

"That's okay. It's kind of ingrained in me."

"Well, out-grain it. Because you and I are competition."

Clearly surprised, he said, "What?"

Holding the gaze of his sexy pale eyes, she decided a strong dose of truth wouldn't just get rid of her attraction. It would also put his guard up so this would be a fair fight. She might need to get the vineyard into Giordano hands again, but she wouldn't cheat, lie or steal. That had been Adam's forte.

"I fully intend to buy this vineyard back from you."

His brow furrowed. "But I just bought it."

"My dad put it up for sale prematurely."

"No. Your dad picked the right time. I saw the

books. Had he waited even another three months, penalties and interest would have bankrupted him."

"Yes, well. I had a source for the money. He should have talked to me, not gone to you."

He crossed his arms on his chest. The blue eyes behind the lenses of his glasses narrowed. "If you had a source for the money, why didn't you bail your dad out *before* he came to me?"

"My friend Janine's mother became ill suddenly, and I couldn't contact her about a loan. That would have been inappropriate."

He lowered his arms. "Oh." But the skepticism hadn't left his voice when he said, "This friend has an extra thirty million dollars hanging around?"

"Actually, she could probably lend me ten times that and not miss it."

His voice hardened. "And how do you intend to pay it back?"

"Profits from the vineyard—and before you ask, she'll give me an interest rate much lower than the bank, making the payments manageable."

He said only, "Hmm," and then he motioned to the door for her to walk outside ahead of him. But he stopped suddenly and said, "Wait a second."

He took off his jacket and tossed it to the bench with a bag that was probably his. Then he loosened his tie. As his hands worked the knot, the fringe of a sleeve tattoo appeared at his wrist.

Her breath caught a little.

She forced air into her lungs, stopping that reaction before it really started. She couldn't be attracted to him. The notion was idiotic. A romance—even a casual affair—was the last thing she wanted or needed right now. Especially with an American like Adam had been. Educated. Gorgeous. Except where Adam had been blond, Trace had black hair. And she'd bet he had dark chest hair and six-pack abs—

This time the wave that hit her was disbelief at her own stupidity. Hadn't falling for one smooth-talking American been enough? Hadn't losing all the money her family had borrowed to pay for the new building taught her a lesson?

A year might have passed, but she still felt the sting of it. She was only now coming back to herself. She wouldn't wreck that over a handsome face.

Sexy or not, Trace Jackson was the opposition. Not quite an enemy but the guy who had her family's business. And she had to wrestle it back—even as she trained him enough that he would see he didn't really want to own a vineyard. Running one wasn't as romantic and easy as everyone thought. The work was hard, hours were long, and tourists weren't always pleasant.

As they made the short walk to the wine building, he rolled his white shirtsleeves to his elbows. Refusing to allow herself a quick look at his tattoos, she opened the door on two long mahogany bars with round tables scattered throughout the sparkling-clean room. The gift shop behind a wall of glass at the far right held everything from single bottles of wine to wineglasses with the silver-and-white vineyard logo, as well as towels, mugs, stoppers and T-shirts, all displayed as if they were fine jewels. Everything about the room screamed sophistication. If it didn't shine like well-polished wood, it glowed from a recent scrubbing.

It was perfect as the initial thing tourists saw. She'd made sure of that, cradling the project with loving hands. Handling every detail. Thinking through every tile and piece of machinery.

Trace strolled the room, smiling, the gorgeous artwork of the tattoos on his forearms revealed for all the world to see. He hadn't gone to the back room of a bar in his city for his art. No. His tattoos had been drawn by a master.

"This room is what sold me on buying the vineyard."

Marcia smiled stiffly. Not merely because it rankled that someone had bought her baby, but because one of those weird whooshes of attraction had roared through her again, causing her blood to tingle and her knees to turn to jelly. A businessman with tattoos? What could be sexier?

She had to take a breath before she could say, "Really?"

He ambled around the silent room, his movements smooth and incredibly male. Especially with his sleeves rolled up.

Annoyed with herself, she forced her eyes away. It didn't matter how sexy he was. He wouldn't be staying.

"This space was filled with tourists the day I walked through with your dad."

Which explained why Marcia hadn't seen him. Her father had probably deliberately mixed him in with the crowd so he wouldn't be noticed. The vineyard's financial troubles had bruised Antonio Giordano's pride, and she knew he blamed her, no longer trusted her and hadn't wanted her opinions. Not even on the sale of the business that was to be her future.

"Everyone was happy, praising the samples they tasted." Trace turned to face her again. "And orders for cases of Giordano's finest flowed as naturally and as freely as the wine."

"We have a very good reputation."

"And I want to make sure that reputation stays intact. That's the wine's biggest selling point. The vineyard's reputation. That's why I won't be renaming it Jackson Vineyards or Trace of Delight Wines."

A spontaneous laugh burst from Marcia and she cut it off. The man was charming and easygoing. But that didn't matter. *Couldn't* matter.

He walked over, met her gaze. "If you intend to

buy me out because you're worried that I'm going to change things, I'm not. I'm a CPA. I know a good deal when I see one. This vineyard is a success. Your dad would have never sold it had it not been for the embezzling."

Her heart stopped. Her breath froze.

He knew about Adam?

Of course he did. A smart businessman would investigate every nook and cranny of the vineyard's history...and its accounting...before buying.

The sale might have been fast, and she might not have been told about it until agreements had already been signed, but she hadn't been made general manager because she was pretty. She'd been educated to build Giordano Wines. She knew business. Some part of her had always realized the new owner would find out about the embezzling. She simply hadn't acknowledged it until this minute.

But now that she had, she would breathe again. Really.

She forced air in and out of her lungs, accepting the fact that her greatest mistake was a part of the vineyard's history. She'd never escape it. It would follow her like an unwashed dog.

"Anyway, we both know I understand numbers. What I don't know is wine." He pointed to the double aluminum doors in the middle of the far wall. "Let's take a look back there."

Relief that he didn't ask for details about the

embezzling poured through her, quelling the wild beating of her heart. Then she realized he'd asked a few questions and moved on as if he either didn't take her seriously about buying the vineyard back from him or didn't see her as a threat.

Something hot and angry flickered through her. *This* she wouldn't ignore. This she would handle.

CHAPTER TWO

TRACE FOLLOWED MARCIA to the destemmer, a little clearer about what was going on with her. She was furious that her dad had sold the vineyard out from under her. He would have been too. But he wasn't done figuring her out. It was farfetched that she had a friend who could lend her the money to buy it back. A thirty-million-dollar loan was a huge favor. More than that, he couldn't understand why she'd want to put herself in that much debt.

She motioned toward the back of the building, to big garage doors. "Grapes come in there. Washed over there. And are brought here for destemming, then poured into the crusher."

Impressed by how new everything was, he inspected the silent machine.

Marcia continued her explanation. "Wine is a five-step process. Picking the grapes, crushing the grapes, fermenting the grapes into wine, aging the wine and bottling the wine. It's not difficult to learn."

He peered over at her. "There might only be five steps, but there are steps within those steps."

She nodded. "Seeds and skin are removed. Yeast is added. But if we take this one process at a time, after we pick the grapes in late summer, early fall, you'll see every step inside each process."

"So, your plan to buy me out is long term? You're not going to hand me a check tomorrow?"

She shrugged. "I'm trying to be fair."

Plus, she didn't have the money. At least not yet. "Fair?"

"I'll give you a whole year to see the process. So, you can make an informed decision. But I'm betting you'll be out sooner."

He had to hold back a chuckle. Working with a woman who intended to oust him might not be smart, but she wasn't a threat. She couldn't take back the vineyard without him selling it to her. Plus, she knew how to run this place and he didn't. Add in that she was pretty and just miffed enough to be interesting, and this conversation was the best fun he'd had in years. Most things in life were easy to him. Even buying Giordano Vineyards had been nothing but a little research and writing a check. He was thrilled that it came with a puzzle.

He liked puzzles.

"Winemaking isn't as easy as it sounds."

He wandered around the room. "Oh, I get that.

Following steps is one thing. But experience, instinct is quite another."

"Exactly."

"And you think I'm going to flub that?"

When she said nothing, he recognized she was smart enough to see he was baiting her and she pulled back. Which was a point in her favor. She might be angry, but she knew how to control it. He decided it was time to be as honest with her as she was being with him. At his old company he'd been known as The Eliminator because he didn't fuss around. He got things out in the open and dealt with them.

"It will take years before I admit defeat. Up to then, I'll just consider myself in the learning curve. I'll never sell this back to you."

"Why don't we cross that bridge when we come to it?"

"Because I'm trying to be as fair as you are, to let you see what you're up against if you seriously think you'll get this vineyard back. I'm a planner. My friends and I owned a huge holding company for supermarket chains. We didn't get to that size by leaving anything to chance."

She frowned. "A holding company for supermarket chains?"

"Enormous corporation. Massive five-year plans and forecasts. Tons of work. This vineyard will be just enough mental stimulation to entertain me and not so much as to make me crazy."

"Your other company made you crazy?"

"No. Not having anything to do after we sold it made me crazy." He wouldn't tell her that having too much time to think about the pain of the past had driven him home. Hoping a visit with his down-to-earth parents would soothe him, he'd brought gifts and planned to stay a few weeks. But his father had made a comment about his son, how everything had worked out for the best after his death, and Trace had melted inside. How could the death of his innocent baby and the end of his teenage marriage have been for the best? He lived with a permanent hole in his heart and a head full of unanswered questions and his parents didn't know what to say, couldn't soothe him. Even now, the memory of his lost child crushed his chest, made it hard to breathe.

He couldn't go back twelve years and change things or even ease the pain, so he'd decided to go forward. Buying this vineyard and moving to Italy was such a huge step, it would shift his thoughts, occupy his brain, calm him again.

He was sure of it.

Marcia's voice tiptoed into the silent room. "If having nothing to do makes you crazy, why did you sell your company?"

He glanced at her, blinking to bring himself back to the present. "Actually, my partners and I received an offer out of the blue. It was higher than any of us believed we'd ever get. We cashed out and became wealthy in the process." He let his gaze cruise the room again. "We'd have been fools not to take it."

He ambled around a bit more, liking the feel of the place and the knowledge that the challenge of running the vineyard would easily get his mind off his past. Then the peace of the area would surely help him get more than an hour or two of sleep every night.

"But that's when I realized too much time on my hands wasn't a good thing. I wanted something to do but not something as extreme as running ten grocery store chains. Almost two hundred stores. Thousands of employees."

"That's a lot of accounting."

He laughed. "It was intense."

She sniffed. "You could have hired people to help."

"Oh, we did," he said, strolling around the big silver machine. "Let's just say you don't get rich by paying other people to do what you can do." He grinned stupidly. "And I like to work."

"Just not too hard."

He laughed again. He should have been annoyed by her impertinence, but he liked her. She had just enough sass to be good as a manager and not so much that she hadn't known to shut up when he baited her.

"Agreed. I like to work, but not too hard."

Her expression soured.

"Sorry to disappoint you."

"Oh, you don't disappoint me. I didn't think it would be easy to get you to sell. But you'll sell." She met his gaze. "I guarantee it."

The competitive streak in him sat up. "So, this is like a bet?"

"No."

"A competition, then? You think you can get me to sell. I think I can get you to like working for me enough that you'll stay on after the year is up." He smiled. "Maybe indefinitely."

"Never happen."

He laughed. "Seriously? Don't tell me that. That just fires my blood. Now for sure I'll beat you."

She held out her hand. "So, what do you say we set terms? If I can't get you to sell, I'll stay on for five years."

Impressed, he considered that. Five years would give him plenty of time to learn how to make wine. Then if she wanted to leave, it wouldn't be a hardship. He reached to shake the hand she held out to him. "Deal."

She drew it back. "Not so fast. If you decide to sell at any time in those five years, you sell only to me…and at three-quarters of the price you paid."

He whistled. "I'll lose twenty-five percent of my investment?"

"That's the deal. Take it or leave it."

He studied her. Five years with her working for

him? Teaching him? He'd have no reason to sell. The three-quarters price was irrelevant.

"Deal."

This time when he reached for her hand, she let him take it. When their palms met, electricity shimmied up his arm.

He ignored it. He might be attracted to this brunette, but now they had a bet for the piece of property that was supposed to give him back his sanity.

Not that he thought he'd lose. Her terms were too broad and general. All he had to do was stay owner of the vineyard for five years. Which had been his plan anyway.

One gorgeous, smart Italian woman wouldn't send him packing. Not when he needed the peace and tranquility and the challenge of the bet more than he needed the money.

She took a breath, turned on her heel and walked away.

He stifled a laugh. If she thought treating him poorly would get him to sell, that was adorable. He loved puzzles and competitions. His brain thrived on them. The more she tried to make this diffi-cult, the sharper he'd get and the happier he'd be. And thoughts of his past would all but disappear. She'd just made this deal perfect.

The rest of the afternoon passed quickly, with Marcia showing Trace every piece of equipment,

the vats, the store
tion, but now th
all but glowed

Tired at the
through the
bag, and w

His brea
the hall
but ther
five on the n
peace and serenity
at his fingertips.

Well, he had no idea
bang. But it was lou
He raced down
now a bunch of
the kitchen to
a tank top, lo
cook.
His br
the lon
kitch

Happy, he showered and dresse
an oversize T-shirt. The plan was to hop
Maserati and cruise into town for dinner, then
a trip to the market for essentials like eggs and
bread. He'd bartered with the Giordano family
to leave behind some dishes and pots and pans,
so all he needed were a few basics. When he returned, he would grab a bottle of wine made at *his*
vineyard and settle in on the back patio to bask in
his new reality. He would listen to night sounds,
savor his wine, then go to bed in the peace and
quiet of Tuscany.

And hopefully, he'd sleep.

As he stepped out of the master bedroom, a
noise drifted to him. Thinking it might have been
the house creaking, he walked down the stairs to
the foyer, but he heard another sound. This one
was odd like…

. It wasn't quite a crash or a
d and coming from the back.
the hall, following what was
lattering noises, and strode into
ind Marcia, dressed in jeans and
oking like she was getting ready to

ow furrowed as she glanced at him over
island of the white and stainless-steel
en.

I guessed you would want me to make dinner."

"Can you…? *Should* you?" Holy cow, she
looked great. She might be small, but her body
packed a punch. Her tank top didn't merely show
off ample bosoms; it cinched her tiny waist.

His thoughts paused, then backed up a bit.

She'd changed clothes and was in the kitchen?
Why hadn't she gone home?

Why was she comfortably searching for pots…
as if she—?

"Is there food in the fridge?"

She shrugged. "A bit. Mama left a few things."

"Like to make your lunch while you're working?"

She winced. "That and a bit more."

His stomach fell. "Are you still living here?"

She frowned. "I've always lived here."

"Until I bought this house. Then it became mine
and your family moved out."

"Oh. I see." She chuckled. "You think because

my family has gone, I should have gone." She shook her head. "But no. You kept me on as the employee I've always been, and I've always lived here. Meaning room and board come with the deal I've always had as an employee here." She smiled. "But, if you think about it, if I'm buying you out, there's no point in my moving anyway."

"There's plenty of point! Per our deal, I'm staying at least five years. And I bought this vineyard for peace and quiet. Having somebody live with me sort of ruins that." And was nonnegotiable. If she thought he'd gotten soft because he'd taken her bet, she was wrong. Trace Martin Jackson wasn't soft.

The Eliminator in him came roaring to life. If her living here was part of her plan to edge him out, she had opened a can of worms she should have left closed.

She shook her head. "You think you're staying, but grape harvest might scare you off. It gets rowdy."

"Rowdy?" He walked toward her, but the closer he got the more his nerve endings prickled. He enjoyed a good fight, but these prickles were different. More like prickles of attraction than getting his hackles up to take on the enemy.

He stopped, casually took two steps back, not liking the way the attraction kept weaving between them anytime they were in a room together. "Rowdy won't intimidate me."

"All right. How about this? Guests aren't here only from nine to five. They can stay into the night. It'll be handy to have me around."

His brain stalled. He hadn't thought of that. Mostly because he didn't know anything about running a vineyard. "Okay." Because he didn't want her thinking she'd won, he added, "I'm not getting soft. I simply see your point. Being over-confident about getting me to change my mind will get you into trouble."

She laughed as if she thought him wrong, but when she grabbed a pot handle again, weirdness about her cooking brought The Eliminator back, the guy who saw and solved problems. She might be sleeping in his house that night, but she was still an employee and he would not open himself up to a lawsuit because she thought he "assumed" she would cook. *After hours.* While they were *living together.*

No. This was a problem he would fix immediately.

"You're not cooking."

"What?"

"You're an employee. You're not cooking for the boss." To soften the blow, he added, "I'll take you out for dinner."

She stopped dead in her tracks. "In town?"

"Sure. We can get something to eat, then go to the market, pick up a few things like coffee, cream, eggs, bread and whatever else I think of."

She only stared at him.

Either she really, really liked to cook or she was so accustomed to making her own dinner, she appeared stymied by having a choice. But he wasn't risking a lawsuit. As long as they worked together, she would not cook.

"I can't let you prepare meals for me. I don't know how things are here in Italy, but bosses don't take advantage of employees in the US. Unless they like lawsuits."

"I know. I went to school in the States." She sighed. "It's just that—" Confusion filled her face. Then she rolled her eyes. "Oh, whatever." Setting the pan on the counter, she said, "Let's go."

They walked to his car in silence with him feeling like he'd dodged a bullet about potential lawsuits, until he realized she might have hesitated because she didn't want to go to dinner with *him*. After all, he was her boss. He'd bought her family's vineyard. And they'd already spent a whole darned afternoon together. If nothing else, she was probably sick of him.

He wanted to groan. He'd been so sure when he'd met her that he could figure her out. Then she'd lured him into a bet and now he seemed to have lost his ability to decipher a normal situation.

He almost told her she didn't have to go, but before he got the words out she was in the car. He decided to make the evening fun, to get to know her, and hopefully establish a less confusing work relationship.

They couldn't talk on the drive to town because of the noise of having the car's top down. But as soon as he stopped the engine in the parking lot of a quaint tavern, he said, "This is such a nice little village."

She smiled stiffly. "Yes. It's lovely."

Okay. Getting her to talk might take a bit of work, but he'd faced grumpier employees before.

He opened the thick wooden door of the tavern, but when they entered, the prickly sensation of being watched rolled down his spine. Not only did all eyes turn in their direction, but people stopped talking as they walked to one of the empty tables.

He realized they could be curious about him—the new guy in town—until he saw the waitress get the bartender's attention and point at Marcia.

He winced. He might be new in town, but that went only so far in terms of gossip and curiosity. Marcia's family, on the other hand, had lost their vineyard under truly gossip-worthy circumstances. From the guarded expression on Marcia's face, he knew she felt every eye on her.

He pulled out her chair, then his. "So, this is a nice place."

She looked neither right nor left. She kept her eyes down. And he felt like hell. *This* was why she'd hesitated to come out with him. It had been a year since her employee had vanished with their loan money, but people in this town had long memories. Or maybe nothing more exciting had happened in the twelve months that had passed.

"Every place in Tuscany is beautiful."

Her subdued voice went through him like a knife. Why had he insisted she come with him? He could have let her cook her own meal, gone into town for dinner alone and gone to the market without her. But, no... His big brain always had a plan.

To lighten the mood, he said, "You sound like you should be on their tourism board."

She laughed and he breathed an internal sigh of relief. Then the waitress came over.

"*Ciao*, Marcia!" The smirky little smile she gave Marcia set Trace's teeth on edge. "What can I get you?"

"I'll have a beer," Trace said before Marcia could answer. He'd been the victim of gossip. Whispers. Speculation. Out-and-out lies. He remembered going into the town convenience store the week after Skylar discovered she was pregnant. The hushed shoppers. The clerk who gave him a wide-eyed stare, as if no one else in the world had ever gotten pregnant at eighteen. The gossip that her wealthy parents were furious and looking for ways to get Skylar away from him.

Unfortunately, that part was true.

The waitress laughed. "Beer in wine country?"

"American beer, if you have it." There. If she wanted something to snipe about, he'd just given it to her. "We'll have wine with our meal. Could we have menus?"

The waitress said, "Of course," and sped away.

"That was Gina. She's—"

"A real pain in the butt." Trace finished her sentence with truth to get everything out in the open. That was another thing he'd learned about gossip. Truth usually killed it. "Look, we both know the circumstances surrounding my getting your family's vineyard weren't the best. And you were general manager when one of your employees stole from your family."

Playing with the silverware on the table, Marcia said nothing.

"You shouldn't run. You shouldn't hide. Clearly everybody knows. Let it ebb and flow until it dies out. The more you react, the longer it lives."

She stared at her silverware for a few seconds, then finally looked him in the eyes. "It sounds like you have some experience with gossip."

He winced. Walked right into that one. "That's a story for another time." Or never. Most people could barely remember what they'd done at eighteen. They didn't have to confess getting the daughter of the town rich guy pregnant, talking her into running away and getting married, having a child, losing that child and then divorcing so quickly he wasn't sure either he or Skylar had had a chance to grieve.

He'd taken that loss to community college, drunk a little too much some nights, then finally realized it was better to drown himself in his studies than whiskey. Which was why he'd eventually gotten into Harvard and why he'd become wealthy. He really had learned things.

"Right now, you're having dinner with your boss. He's thanking you for teaching him the winemaking process... And if you were smart, you'd take advantage of the opportunity to get on his good side."

Marcia laughed, and then she winced. Protectiveness raced through him but so did anger. He'd heard the story of the embezzling from her father, but hearing it was totally different from seeing the living, breathing person who took responsibility for it.

She shook her head. "We're in a fierce competition, remember?"

"True. But I love a challenge."

She leaned forward, braced her arms on the table. "Same here."

"That doesn't mean we can't take breaks from it."

Gina returned to the table with two bottles of beer and two menus.

"Not that Marcia needs a menu," the waitress

said pleasantly. "She used to come here all the time. Not quite so sociable now."

Marcia's face reddened and Trace thought he'd go through the roof with anger. Gina's snide comments reminded him of his own past again, the insults, the insinuations that the kid in worn sneakers and ripped jeans had wanted a cut of Skylar's family's money, and the fake condolences when his son died.

Gina left to give them time to look at the menu and Trace said, "Forget all that. You have a much more interesting dinner companion. I might have started out in community college, but I got my MBA from Harvard." He smiled at her. "Go ahead. Pick my brain."

Before she could answer, he glanced down at the menu and his eyes widened. "Oh, my gosh!"

"What?"

"Our wine is here. They serve our wine!"

"It's good business for both us and the tavern. We give them a discount. They direct people to our vineyard."

His eyes glowed. "No. You're missing the point. The company my friends and I owned didn't have products. We were sellers of someone else's goods. This," he said, pointing at the segment of the menu offering Giordano wines, "is mine... Ours," he corrected, acknowledging that he hadn't actually been in on the process yet.

Her frown deepened.

He shook his head and leaned back in his chair. His empathy for her was off the charts, but having lived through something painful himself, he knew she had to let go. Maybe he could help her with that as she taught him how to make wine and run a vineyard.

"Come on. Humor me. This is cool, and I'm sorry, but I'm enjoying it."

"You're allowed to enjoy it."

He grinned. Her acknowledging that was a good first step. He needed to keep her going in that direction. Acceptance sprinkled with forward momentum. "Thanks. I know it probably seems to you like I took advantage of your family's bad luck, but I feel like a kid at Christmas."

"Okay. Now you're pushing it."

"Not really. I'm happy. And you could be too. You seem to have a plan to buy me out." His grin widened. "What more could you want?"

She laughed. "Stop being charming. I don't want to like you."

The little zing of pleasure he got when she said she liked him surprised him. He ignored that in favor of his mission of helping her. "I think you simply don't *want* to be happy. You could put that waitress in her place just by laughing and having a good time."

"I don't want to make a scene."

"A good old-fashioned scene is exactly what you need." When she shook her head, he sighed.

"Look, I know that having one of your employees steal from you had to be embarrassing. Maybe even humiliating. But a year's gone by. It almost seems like not letting yourself be happy is your self-imposed penance."

She pulled in a breath. He clearly believed he had her all figured out, but he'd only nipped the tip of the iceberg. Her humiliation wasn't the issue. It was her dad's. Trace kept mentioning that an employee had stolen from them, which probably meant her dad hadn't explained that she'd been *engaged* to that employee.

"There's more to it than that."

"Then tell me."

The exhausted part of her wanted to confide in him. He was a nice guy. Someone who seemed to understand. It might feel good to unburden herself. But he was also the competition. Someone so confident that he'd risked one-quarter of what he'd paid for the vineyard.

All this kindness could all be a trick.

She fiddled with her silverware. "Maybe *that's* a story for another time."

He grimaced. "Got me."

She only smiled, though it was beginning to soak in that what he said was true. She *was* holding back, letting people talk about her, because she felt she deserved it. It might be time to get beyond that, but she couldn't forget her father's shame. Antonio Giordano had lost the vineyard he'd bought when he was a young man and nursed into a thriving business. She'd run it successfully for three years before she'd talked him into expanding and both had realized they needed more help in the office. Another accountant. She'd chosen Adam.

No matter how she sliced it, it was her fault, but her dad's disgrace. Keeping herself as the focus of the incident protected her dad.

Still, Trace's encouragement bolstered her. He eased the dinner conversation back to the vineyard, giving her a chance to display her knowledge, and she wondered if he hadn't done that on purpose too.

She thought of the men she knew...her dad, her brothers, even Adam. Not one of them would have even noticed the humiliation that surrounded her. Yet Trace had.

The drive back to the vineyard with the top down on his Maserati was heavenly and she wondered how she'd been so preoccupied that she hadn't noticed that on the ride into town. The wind lifted her hair, swirled around her. She would never, ever, ever forget how her mistakes had embarrassed her dad—shamed him. But for the twenty minutes it took to get from town to the villa, she let peace wash through her.

She walked to the front door as Trace grabbed his bags from the tiny trunk of his sports car. She hit the code sequence on the keypad of the lock and opened the door. In the kitchen, she helped him stow the coffee, cream, eggs, milk and bread in various places.

With everything done, she wiped her hands down her jeans. "I guess I'll see you in the morning."

He nodded. "See you in the morning."

They both walked out of the kitchen, through the hall, into the foyer and up the stairs.

He winced. "This is awkward."

She tried to laugh but it came out stiff. Knowing he was behind her, his eyes about level with her butt, sent tingles and possibilities careening through her.

"Yeah. We could have saved our good-nights."

"We *should have* saved our good-nights. At least then we wouldn't have been walking in silence."

Glad when they hit the upstairs hall, she marched to her bedroom door. "Good night," she called, thinking he'd walk past her.

He stopped. "Yeah. Good night." He grinned. "Again."

Their situation was funny but not that funny. "You're enjoying this owning-a-vineyard thing a little too much."

"I can't help it. I needed some peace and quiet and now I own it."

It wasn't his first mention that he wanted peace

and quiet, but it was the first time she realized there might be a crack in his armor, a reason he longed for peace and tranquility...thousands of miles away from his home. A reason he understood her troubles.

She studied his face, seeing lines she hadn't noticed before.

"I had a great time. Thank you for making my first night a weird kind of celebration."

She remembered how difficult the beginning of their dinner had been. How he'd labored to bring her out of her shell. Such a strange and interesting man. Desperate for privacy, even as he seemed to be clicking with her.

Holding his gaze, looking for answers, she said, "You're weird if you think that dinner was a celebration."

He smiled. "It was just right. Enough wine and conversation to begin my new life."

The *new life* comment raised her curiosity again. He'd helped her that night. Now he was saying she'd helped him. Maybe she wasn't the only one reaching for something.

That was when she realized how close they were standing. As if being drawn together by some unseen force, they'd inched nearer and nearer until they were close enough to kiss.

Their gazes locked and warmth flooded her, along with a quick, quiet wish that he'd touch his lips to hers. She could see in his eyes that he wanted to, and she'd been alone for so long she could barely remember what it felt like to be desired. Their dinner had been the best evening she'd had in forever. An accidental date—

The mere thought of a date with him shot fear through her. Wouldn't she be the biggest loser of all time to fall twice for someone who came to the vineyard?

She would.

She backed away, swiped her gaze across his. Too bad. She sensed he really was nice, but not too nice. More like honest. He seemed to like to deal with people frankly. Plus, he had a story. No one got to be as empathetic as he was without having gone through something himself. She could probably help him as much as he could help her.

But there was always that risk. She wasn't known for being the best judge of character and any guesses she had about him were just that. Guesses.

She turned to her bedroom door. "Good night."

"Good night."

She walked into her room and closed the door softly, not wanting to alert him to the fact that he'd thrown her off her game. But he had. She'd noticed him, sensed things about him, been curious, interested...happy.

All things she was no longer allowed to be.

Not that she intended to be a workaholic for the rest of her life. It was more that she wouldn't permit herself pleasure until she fixed the problems she'd made for her dad.

She kicked off her shoes as she slid her phone out of the back pocket of her jeans. Hitting Contacts, she searched for Janine's phone number, then let it dial.

Voice mail answered and Marcia's heart stuttered. The way Janine's phone went straight to the recording could be a hint that her mother's condition had worsened. It felt forward to leave a message with such a mundane request. Money might be Marcia's top priority, but that didn't hold a candle to Janine's mother's cancer.

She thought for a second, realizing the voice mail answer could be a matter of time zones or Janine simply being busy. She could even be in the shower. Her call might not be an intrusion at all.

After a deep breath, she said, "Hey, Janine, it's Marcia. I'm hoping things have improved with your mom and I'm so sorry I can't be there with you. I wanted to talk to you, and I know you have other things going on but… We have a little problem at the vineyard. Remember how you've always said you'd be happy to lend me the money to start a business?" She swallowed hard, then trudged on. Trace was a little too charming and she was a little too vulnerable to wait too long with her request. She hated bothering Janine with this, but maybe things had gotten better for her mom. Or maybe Janine needed a diversion.

"I could use that money now." She laughed a bit, trying to dislodge the lump in her throat. "When you have time, give me a call, please."

She hung up feeling like a heel. And why not? She'd trusted Adam, brought him into her family, didn't pay attention to the way her father was beginning to also trust him too much, and he stole from them.

Now she was asking a friend for money at a really bad time for Janine.

How could one mistake, trusting the wrong man, have upended her entire life?

CHAPTER THREE

THE NEXT MORNING, Trace was sitting on the back patio, enjoying his coffee and reading the news on his phone, when he heard the sound of Antonio Giordano's old red truck chugging down the driveway. Right on time. Matteo and Roberto, Antonio's sons, were arriving to run the wine room and teach Trace the ropes.

He set his cup on the table as he slid his phone into his back pocket. By the time he reached the front of the villa, Antonio and his two sons had piled out of the truck.

"*Buongiorno*, Signor Jackson!"

"*Buongiorno*, Antonio!" He was a little confused about why Antonio had arrived but thought maybe he'd simply driven his sons to work.

Antonio pointed to two tall, strapping young men. Both dressed in black trousers and white shirts with sleeves rolled to the elbows, both with curly dark hair. "These are my sons, Matteo and Roberto, who will work for you until the end of the year, per our agreement."

Matteo and Roberto stepped forward to shake his hand. Trace could easily see these two handsome guys flirting with tourists, getting them to open their wallets and buy wine. But also giving the vineyard a reputation for being a fun place, which translated to lots of stars on the review sites.

"After that," Antonio said, "you and the boys will either negotiate to continue their employment or they can move on."

"Yes. That was the deal," Trace said, glad Antonio had come with his sons for the introductions, but his curiosity grew when the older man headed for the wine building. "You're staying?"

Antonio stopped and turned. "I hope you don't mind. I thought you might need some help on your first day. Someone to explain things."

True. He probably would.

"That's great. Thanks."

Antonio started toward the door again. "The first bus of tourists is scheduled to arrive at nine. But stragglers who rent cars can show up at any time all day."

Rushing ahead to beat Antonio to the door, Trace opened it, granting entry to the three Giordano men. "Good to know."

Antonio nodded and Trace walked into the wine room, taking a long drink of air, so happy to be starting his new life that he hated the odd feeling having Antonio around gave him. First,

Marcia thought she should get room and board because that was the way it had always been. Now, Antonio was in the wine-tasting room, almost as if he couldn't let go of his old job.

Telling himself to stop being territorial, Trace decided he should look at this in a more positive light. As long as Antonio was at the vineyard, he could pal around with him and learn his role as the happy vintner.

The men walked to the long bar. Behind them, the door opened again, and Trace turned to see Marcia stepping into the wine-tasting room. He hadn't seen her at breakfast, which was basically toast and coffee. She looked amazing in a sleeveless dress that displayed the perfection of her figure.

Attraction rolled through him, but he reminded himself that she had troubles. He might have tried to help her the night before, but after his strange, jumbled feelings at her bedroom door, he wasn't sure getting too close was a good idea. She was an employee. He couldn't be attracted to her.

She smiled at her father. "Papa, I see you and Trace are already getting things set up."

Antonio stepped back, looking away from Marcia. "We're fine. Go to the office and do whatever it is you do back there."

Marcia's spine stiffened but she kept her smile firmly in place. "There is always plenty of work."

She walked to the steel doors behind the tasting bar, pushed through and disappeared.

Trace faced Antonio. "I guess there are offices back there."

Antonio straightened. His eyes narrowed. "She did not show you?"

"She showed me a ton of things yesterday, Antonio." He'd seen the coolness Antonio had for Marcia, but he also saw something more. Maybe a desire to catch her doing something wrong? Trace didn't know. But he didn't like it. Still, he filed it away to think about later. He wasn't letting anything ruin his first real day as a vintner.

"I'm sure she intended to show me the offices today."

He heard the sound of an engine and tires crunching in the parking lot, and he grinned. "But I think it might be more fun to interact with tourists than to go back and look at the books."

Antonio slapped him on the back. "Then let's go greet your first busload of guests."

Marcia sat at her desk, took a long, calming breath and closed her eyes. She couldn't even muster righteous indignation that her father had embarrassed her. She knew she deserved it.

She stayed out of the wine-tasting area, giving her dad space to enjoy the day with Trace. At five o'clock, she left her office through the back entry and headed to the house. She'd checked her phone a hundred times that day, but there had been no call from Janine.

When she reached her bedroom door, she had an unexpected thought about living here. Her belief about room and board coming with her job might have been valid, but she suddenly wondered if she shouldn't begin searching for an apartment. She hated the idea of moving out of the villa, then moving back, but she had to admit she was attracted to Trace. The night before, standing at her bedroom door, odd feelings kept buzzing between them, tempting her.

She could get past the fact that he was good-looking. She could enjoy his sense of humor and walk away. But those were surface things. There was more to him than met the eye and half of his allure was the fact that she'd have to dig to find the real Trace. The other half was a blissful suspicion that the struggle would be worth it.

She stopped her thoughts, reminding herself she had a job to do—get the vineyard back from him. She chuckled, thinking of the hard work of grape harvest, and envisioned her family in the villa, where they belonged, at Christmastime.

Surely, she could keep her wits about her for six months.

A little after eight o'clock her stomach growled. With the rental cars and buses now gone from the parking lot, she knew her father and brothers would soon be going home, and Trace would be coming in for dinner.

Remembering their meal from the night before, the awkwardness at the tavern, she grabbed a pot from a cabinet beneath the center island, filled it with water and found some of her mother's pasta and a jar of sauce that had been saved from the last big batch her mama made.

By the time Trace came into the kitchen, looking freshly showered, with his dark hair slicked back, the pasta had finished cooking and the sauce was warm.

She smiled, determined to get them back to a normal working relationship, even if they did live together. "How do you feel about penne for dinner? Mama left a few jars of her homemade sauce behind."

He groaned. "That sounds heavenly." He walked to the stove and sniffed the sauce. "Oh, God." His stomach growled. "I didn't eat lunch. Didn't want to miss a minute of watching your brothers sweet-talk tourists."

She laughed. "Yeah. That can be fun."

He shook his head. "Damn, your brothers are good. I don't think I'll ever be that smooth."

She poured the drained pasta into a big bowl. "I'm sure you would be." She sneaked a peek at him. She could be normal, but she would also keep him on the ropes. Reminding him that they were adversaries would prevent either of them from paying too much attention to their attraction and crossing any lines. "If you were staying."

"Oh, I'm staying. And I'm starving. I'm not going to say no to penne and homemade sauce." He walked to another cupboard, found two wineglasses and stopped. "Should we eat here? At the island?"

"We could eat outside," she suggested. "There are tables out there."

"Yeah, I know. I was out there last night." He quickly added, "And ate my toast there this morning."

He said both casually, but her senses began to prickle, and she forgot all about keeping him on his toes. Had he gone out there after she'd gone to bed? After *he'd* said good-night and gone to his room?

Her intuition begged her to ask why he wanted the quiet. What had happened in his life? He had a story. She knew he did—

But so did she and she didn't want to tell hers. She'd think long and hard before she tried to pry his from him.

He left to get a bottle of wine, and when he returned, he said, "I just want to go on the record and say I didn't ask you to make dinner."

"Still worried about lawsuits?"

"Is cooking in your job description?"

"No." She winced. "Mostly because I don't really have a job description. That's the problem with a family-owned business. I did things as a daughter that maybe a normal general manager wouldn't have done. But when your home is your work and your work is your home… I guess that's going to happen."

"So, you did cook?"

"Sure. Mama typically made lunch and dinner for my dad and brothers and for everybody during grape harvest. I would help."

He considered that for a second, then frowned. "I think we need to write job descriptions and add in occasional cooking."

She shook her head, but she chuckled. "Americans. You're so lawsuit happy."

He didn't even try to deny it. "That we are."

"Well, in Italy we're not. And I am living here. It's not out of line for me to cook…or for you to cook."

He snorted. "If I cook, you might not be happy."

"Why don't we let me be the judge of that? Particularly since it's the best way to keep things even between us."

He frowned, as he appeared to think that through. "Okay. All that makes perfect sense."

"Good. Then you won't mind if I tell you to get dishes and utensils while I carry the pasta to the table."

"I will not mind at all."

There was a silliness to his voice that almost stopped her in her tracks. But it was after hours and deep down he was a nice guy. She'd seen it the night before at the tavern with the way he'd helped her cope with Gina and even enjoy the evening.

She picked up the bowl of pasta and took it to the back patio. Well-spaced lighting brightened the place just enough that they could see but not so much that it destroyed the ambience of the warm night. She set the bowl on the table and took the dishes from Trace when he brought them.

"I'm going back in for the wine."

"Good."

By the time he returned, the table had been set and Marcia sat facing the house, leaving the view of the pool and the vineyard for him. He poured her a glass of wine, then took his seat. The air had cooled enough to be comfortable. The scent of the earth wafted around them.

"Beautiful night."

She smiled. "Yes."

She scooped out a plate of pasta for him, then one for herself.

He picked up his fork. "Sorry. But I skipped lunch," he said, reminding her that he'd enjoyed watching her brothers work.

She said, "Matteo and Roberto can be very entertaining," as he took a bite of his pasta and groaned.

"That's fabulous."

"Just some stuff Mama left behind for us."

"I wonder how much I'd have to pay her to leave stuff behind every day."

"She would be thrilled to have you ask."

"Maybe I will."

He ate nonstop for a few minutes, pausing only for wine, and she shook her head. "You really were starving."

"I think it's all the fresh air."

Confused by his appreciation of fresh air, she asked, "Where did you live in the States?"

"Manhattan."

"It's nice there?"

"There is no other place in the world like it. There's big money on Wall Street and penthouses for the people who play with it." He paused, thinking before he said, "Central Park. Broadway. And people everywhere."

"You loved it." She paused, then cautiously added, "Even the noise."

"The first day I stepped out of a taxi onto the sidewalk across from our office building, I knew I was home."

She tilted her head as she studied him. The more she heard, the less she understood. "Yet you are here."

He scooped up more pasta. "I told you. We sold the business."

"And you had too much time to think." Questions about him nagged at her again. But she stifled them, picking up her wine and taking a sip.

The sky had darkened enough that the moon shone through. And her mother's pasta, as always, was delicious.

She'd appreciated this as a family home, but tonight it suddenly felt like a bachelor's lair. Odd how a change of ownership had shifted the entire feel of the place. Of course, the inside was empty, except for the dining room table, kitchen things, her bed and the bed her parents had left behind for him. They'd also left behind the outdoor tables and furniture. But that was it. Beyond that, the huge villa was a blank slate, waiting to be filled.

"We should go to the city to shop for furniture for you sometime."

He lifted his wineglass. "Really? I was thinking about shopping online."

"You could do that," she readily agreed because she wasn't sure why she'd made the suggestion. The moonlight, the wine, the pasta and her curiosity about him seemed to have moved a few of the walls she'd erected around herself.

As simply and naturally as it had happened, though, she didn't like it. It made her feel easy. Desperate. Susceptible to a little moonlight and a normal conversation, when she needed to be on her guard, and concerned with getting the vineyard back...not wondering about his past or his problems.

Done with his pasta, he tossed his napkin beside his plate and smiled across the table at her. "I'm not much of a shopper."

"I'm not either. It's just that the house feels so different."

He refilled their wineglasses, then leaned in. His smile was warm and encouraging when he said, "Really? How?"

A sense of connection wove through her, reminding her that they shouldn't be making friends. "It feels empty."

He laughed. "It *is* empty." He sat back in his seat. "Truth be told, I thought I'd wait until I got a sense of the place before I furnished it."

"It seems like the right thing to do."

He leaned in. Smiled again. An odd, warm smile that made her feel like he could see directly into her soul. "It *is* the right thing to do."

The same longing she'd felt the night before at her bedroom door tugged at her heart. If she leaned in too, she could brush her lips across his. She imagined his mouth as soft and warm. She could envision his eyes growing smoky with need.

Desire wove through her. She took a breath and deliberately sat back, putting space between them, bringing herself back to reality. He was gorgeous and charming. He might not think he was, but there was something about his very casual way of speaking to her that made her feel like she'd known him forever—or had been destined to meet him.

Which was silly, romantic nonsense. Just as imagining kissing him had been. Still, she refused to be too hard on herself for thinking these things. She'd made the biggest mistake a woman could make. She trusted a man enough that he stole from her family. But she'd vowed she would never be that foolish again. And she wouldn't be. The very fact that she recognized these feelings and could fight them proved she wasn't the same naive girl she had been when Adam had arrived at the vineyard.

She finished her wine, leading Trace into a discussion of the area. When her glass was empty, she wasted no time gathering their dishes and utensils and heading inside.

"Good night," she called as she walked through the door. She could feel bad for leaving so abruptly. Maybe she *should* feel bad. But leaving was the way to fight the longing to kiss him and the connection she felt with him. She wasn't merely attracted to him. She was drawn to him. Something about him—maybe the way he listened with real interest—made her want to trust him. Made her curious about him. Pushed her guard down so far, she'd spoken without reserve. Listened with genuine curiosity.

And one night when she least expected it, he *would* kiss her. He'd almost made a move the night before, so her intuition didn't have to go out on a limb to make that assumption. And then what would she do? Cave? Submit? Give in to the luscious longings?

She straightened her spine, trying to remind herself she was strong, but she also remembered how easy the night had been…with him. Because of him. Under any other circumstances, the connection she felt with him would be welcome. But with all her baggage, this guy could be perfect for her and she wouldn't see it because she couldn't afford to be a fool again.

In her bedroom, she pulled her phone from her pocket, intending to put it on her bedside table, but she paused. She wished she would hear from Janine, but the dimming of the patio lights reminded her she'd left Trace alone in the moonlight. They'd be laughing together right now, if she hadn't scrambled away.

Disappointment tightened her chest. She was tired of being desperate. Desperate for money. Desperately working to keep her perspective about a man who intrigued her, when he shouldn't.

She just wanted to be normal again.

CHAPTER FOUR

TRACE STAYED ON the patio a few minutes after Marcia went inside. He finished the bottle of wine they'd started, staring out at vineyards lit only by occasional lights that reminded him of streetlights.

After he was sure she'd be upstairs in her room, he headed in. She'd used the excuse of clearing their dishes to get herself away from their conversation, so he only had to dispose of the empty wine bottle. But he also felt weird again. Just as he'd almost kissed her his first night in the villa, he'd been a little too intimate with her at dinner. He hadn't touched her, but he'd leaned forward when she'd spoken, listening intently, lured by the sound of her beautiful, musical voice.

And that was strange. Not something he did. Not how he behaved. He remembered Skylar leaving him at the hospital after they'd been told their infant son was dead, most likely sudden infant death syndrome, but an autopsy would be performed.

She hadn't turned to him for comfort. Hadn't

stayed to comfort him. She hadn't come to the apartment for the death scene investigation. She hadn't helped him provide their child's clinical history. She'd walked away from him, their marriage...their *child*...without a backward glance.

The pain of it could still paralyze him. Freeze his breathing. Empty his heart.

Was it any wonder he was calculated, careful about his interactions with women? After such a horrible loss, he let himself be attracted only to women who wanted a good time. Marcia might need a good time, but she was a woman with trouble, and he was a guy who just liked to play. Commitment was hard. Losses always followed. So, he didn't commit. Ironically, the strategy that had kept him happy for over a decade would end up hurting her.

He couldn't hurt her. She'd been hurt enough. Her judgment error had cost her family their vineyard. And now her father barely spoke to her. He wouldn't add to that.

Walking through the empty downstairs, he sniffed a laugh. She was right. The house did feel different. But to him the odd sensation was transition. The house itself was shifting from the home of a big family who had lived there for almost thirty years to the home of a single man, looking for solitude. There'd be a huge change in the way he would furnish it. But there also wasn't anywhere to sit.

He turned and went outside again, realizing how ironic it was that a man determined to stay single had bought a family home. A family business. And was interacting with the family.

He'd had a family.

Lost a family.

Lost every piece of a future he'd wanted so badly his heart still sometimes yearned for it.

The past twelve years, he'd spent every minute of every day too busy to dwell on the horrific loss of his child and the breakdown of the marriage he'd loved, but under the big starlit sky, in the silence of the Italian countryside, it was all he seemed to be able to think about.

Exactly the opposite of why he'd bought this vineyard.

Pulling his phone from his back pocket, he lowered himself to the chair he'd vacated only a few minutes before and set up a video call with his two friends. When Wyatt White and Cade Smith appeared on the phone screen, his world righted. He'd met them at Harvard and, though they hadn't known it, they'd saved him, brought him back to life enough that he could eventually help them set up the corporation that had made them all rich.

Rubbing a beard the same shiny black as his hair, Wyatt looked like he'd been awakened from a nap. Blond-haired, blue-eyed Cade wore a fishing vest and held a beer.

Wyatt peered at Trace. "What time is it there? Shouldn't you be asleep?"

"No. It's not that late." Trace leaned back. He wouldn't tell his friends that the months of no work had him thinking about his past and given him insomnia. They might know about his losses, but his son had died and his marriage had ended over a decade ago. They would think him crazy to be overwhelmed by memories now. He would handle it on his own. Plus, he had a whole new business he could talk about with them. A new home. A new country.

"I just realized I should have called you earlier while it was light so I could give you a virtual tour."

"No worries." Cade grinned. "I plan on coming to visit in a few weeks."

"Don't. I only negotiated to keep the furniture in the master bedroom and enough pots, dishes and glasses to be able to survive. There isn't another bed." Well, there was, but Marcia was sleeping in it—

"You should go shopping."

"Yeah. Marcia said I should start looking for furniture."

Wyatt sat up. "Marcia?"

Trace waved him off. "Marcia's the general manager. I negotiated for her and her brothers to stay on for a few months to help me. The brothers handle the wine room, giving out samples, selling wine. Marcia does the books, supervises all the admin."

Cade frowned. "Meaning she was the boss of the employee who embezzled?"

Trace relaxed. Discussing his new business—even the sensitive parts—was much better than discussing his insomnia or his past. "Yes."

Wyatt tapped a pencil on his desk. "Are you sure she's trustworthy?"

"If I wasn't, I'd have sent her packing yesterday when I met her. She knows everything there is to know about this company and its wine. I haven't gotten the story of the embezzler yet, but it's clear the whole town knows it. Whoever he was, it's obvious he bamboozled Marcia."

Cade whistled. "Didn't take you long to get that gossip."

He shrugged. "As I said, the whole town knows. Waitress at the tavern the other night treated her like a soccer ball, kicking her because she was down."

Wyatt scratched his scraggly beard again. "Sounds like a beautiful place you moved to."

"Actually, it is," Trace insisted. "I feel like the Giordano Vineyards trouble is an isolated incident. Which makes it even juicier gossip because bad things don't happen here."

Cade sniffed. "You don't know that. You said yourself you don't have the whole story."

"Yeah, but I have the gist of it. Marcia was the

supervisor for the guy who embezzled. Ultimately, the Giordanos lost their vineyard. Her dad obviously blames her. That's the only reason he could be so angry with her that he barely speaks to her."

Cade came to attention. "Her dad barely talks to her?"

"Emotions are still raw."

Wyatt sat up too. "I thought you said this happened a year ago?"

"It did…but…"

"But?" Cade said.

"But there are still some sensitivities that are obvious when she and her dad are in the same room. They don't talk and the air sort of crackles. That's the part I'm still trying to figure out."

Wyatt pursed his lips. "A place or a person with secrets can bring down even the strongest company."

Suddenly Trace was sorry he'd led them into a discussion of the vineyard. They were taking everything he said the wrong way. "I'm not saying there are secrets."

"But you don't believe you have the whole story?"

Trace's stomach sank. He didn't like the feeling he was getting from his friends, the sense that they were seeing something he'd missed. "You think I should have let her go?"

Cade said, "Once you realized there was something going on that you didn't know, you should have point-blank asked. If you didn't like the answer, you should have fired her."

Wyatt said, "Sorry, Trace. But she sounds like trouble."

Trace stilled. The Eliminator in him *had* come out several times in their initial discussions but she'd tempted him with that bet.

Still, he wasn't often wrong about situations, about people. He did not sense deceit in her. "I don't think *she's* trouble. I think she's *in* trouble. She made a mistake that cost her family too much. And she can't get beyond it because her dad is still angry with her." He smoothed his hand across the back of his neck. "I don't know… I feel like I should help her."

Wyatt's head tilted as if he finally understood. "Ah…"

"Ah?" Trace frowned. "What the hell does 'ah' mean?"

"It means you're up to your normal tricks."

"My normal tricks?"

"Yeah. Mr. Fix-It."

"I'm not Mr. Fix-It. I'm The Eliminator, remember? I don't deal with people's personal problems. I only see and solve business problems. That's why it seems weird that I want to help her."

"Technically, two fighting employees do pertain to your business," Wyatt corrected. "And *you* called yourself The Eliminator. We called you Mr. Fix-It."

Cade said, "You were the one who could walk into a grocery store we'd bought and immediately see how to bring it up to our standards. Sometimes that involved firing a person or two… So we let you call yourself The Eliminator. But, really, you were Mr. Fix-It."

Wyatt snorted. "Which is why your wanting to mend this situation for the poor employee who was bamboozled is right up your alley."

Cade laughed. "You might not be the guy who gets all warm and fuzzy, but you like to fix things."

Trace frowned. If he was a fixer, wanting to help her should feel normal. Yet it didn't. There was something different about it. Something more…personal.

When he finally spoke, it was quietly. "I think what bugs me is that I'm responsible for some of her pain. The vineyard wasn't on the market twenty-four hours before I was in negotiations with her dad. I really did not give her a chance to try to bail them out herself."

"You buying the vineyard saved her family from financial ruin," Cade reminded him.

"Yeah, but it underscored that she made some bad judgment calls—"

"Trace, we've all made bad judgment calls," Wyatt said. "We get beyond them. She will too. But you spending too much time thinking about fixing hers seems like it's taking your focus off where it needs to be."

Trace frowned.

"Did you ever stop to think that if you use all your time trying to reunite two feuding employees, you just might fail or get so exhausted with their drama that you'll run screaming?"

"Are you saying you think they are making me uncomfortable on purpose?"

"Are they?"

His frown deepened. He didn't think so. The Giordanos were straightforward people. For Pete's sake, Marcia had warned him she was going to try to buy the vineyard back. He didn't think she or her dad would deceive him. But they were so casual and spontaneous, they *did* have Trace behaving differently. And he finally heard what Cade and Wyatt were saying. Whatever his reasons for his need to help Marcia, it was taking his focus off where it needed to be. On running the vineyard.

And that he would fix.

Maybe he was Mr. Fix-It after all?

The next morning when Trace arrived in the kitchen for breakfast, Marcia stood by the toaster. Her bread popped, she set it on a plate, slathered it with butter and brought it to a stool by the island.

"Good morning."

"Good morning."

His deep voice skipped along her nerve endings, reminding her of the intimacy in the moonlight the night before. She struggled not to notice how handsome he looked in his dark trousers and white shirt, and almost smiled at the way he'd dressed like her dad and brothers. Fitting in.

Except he had tattoos. That sexy art that made her wonder if the good guy she kept seeing was actually a bad boy at heart.

The back door opened, and her dad stepped inside. Trace glanced from her to her dad and then back to her again.

Not wanting to cause a scene, she looked away as her father walked to the coffeepot.

"Trace, we should have a fine time this morning. Lots of buses scheduled. Lots of wine will be sold."

Trace's eyes narrowed as he studied her but spoke to her dad. "That's good."

Pouring coffee into a cup he could take into the wine room, her dad said, "I think I'm beginning to enjoy this role of being here while not really being responsible."

Trace chuckled. "Yeah, that would be nice. All the entertainment of the wine room with none of the worry." He smiled slightly, peeked at her, then spoke to her dad. "But I am kind of curious about how long you intend to be here. I don't have you on the payroll and I'm not sure the budget can handle taking you on."

Antonio laughed and batted a hand. "I don't

need to be paid. Being here is fun for me. I like you. I'm happy to help you adjust and learn. Come grape harvest, you'll be glad I'm here."

With that, her dad headed out, without saying one word to her. Not even *good morning*. At the door, he looked back at Trace. "See you in the wine room."

It couldn't have been more obvious that he was still angry with her.

Trace's voice tiptoed into the quiet kitchen. "Last night my friends pointed out that I'm spending a lot of my time trying to fix your problems."

She nearly choked on her coffee. "What? No one asked you to fix my problems!"

"As long as you and your dad work for me, and your dad won't talk to you, your feud is my problem. Technically, I have a general manager who cowers every time a coworker is in the room."

Unable to deny that, she stayed quiet.

"When I told Wyatt and Cade about the tension between you and your father, they called me Mr. Fix-It. They said when I would go into a business, I could look around, pinpoint the trouble, and if it was a person, I'd fire that person." He winced. "That's the reason I thought they called me The Eliminator."

"Eliminator?"

"Yes, because I got rid of trouble." He winced again. "Sometimes employees. But here's the thing. You have a problem with your dad. He won't talk to you and that hurts you. But I can't fire you. I need you."

She stiffened. "You certainly don't mince words."

"I never do when it comes to a problem. I believe in facing things head-on. That's why I'm telling you all this. There is a problem. We must fix it."

A bad feeling fluttered through her. She remembered how bossy and calculating he'd been the day she'd met him and realized talking to his friends the night before must have reoriented him to the guy he'd been when he worked with them. "Okay."

"I need you here. You're in the agreement of sale. So are your brothers. Your dad is a different matter. I'd be within my rights to ask him not to come here anymore. But I don't want to." He smiled unexpectedly. "He's right. I do like learning from him. I don't want to ban him from the vineyard. Worse, I don't want *that* to be the next rumor that ripples through town. How I kicked him off the vineyard he'd built."

Neither did she. "That gossip would kill my dad."

"Okay, then, what's *your* solution? You're the general manager. How would you handle two fighting employees?"

She took a breath. She hadn't thought her troubles with her dad affected the business. But how could they not? The vineyard was supposed to be a place of relaxation and fun. She was hardly fun when her dad was around.

"I guess my answer has been to stay away from my dad."

He shook his head. "That isn't working. It's a small company. I feel the tension every time the two of you are in a room, and that's taking everyone's focus off our primary goal…which is to make and sell wine. So, either *you* perk up, stop being hurt by things he says or doesn't say, or I'll have to let your dad go."

She blanched. "There have to be other solutions."

"When it comes to people, there are two solutions. Either you two get along or I get rid of one of you. You want your dad to stay? Then you suck it up. I don't want any sad moods, no sad faces. And for God's sake, stand tall when he's around. You're not a coward. In our very first conversation you told me you were going to buy me out and at a twenty-five percent loss. That's the woman I want running the place."

His toast popped. He smeared it with jam, got himself a cup of coffee and walked outside to the patio table.

She blinked. She'd never thought of this situation from a business perspective, only from the vantage point of having hurt her dad. But Trace was right. A good employee worked to get along.

And she absolutely didn't want him asking her dad not to come over. That would be the last straw. At least with Adam having been her fiancé, all the gossip had been directed at her. If the gossip shifted to her dad? The shame of being asked to leave his own vineyard would be impossible to handle.

Her mama arrived later that morning. The gorgeous dark-haired woman from whom Marcia got her beauty and dark eyes sneaked in the back door that led to Marcia's office and enticed her into the kitchen.

Pulling vegetables from a grocery bag, she said, "Your father tells me Trace Jackson is extremely happy and fun to be around."

Which was exactly why she didn't want her dad to leave. He was enjoying himself. Forgetting his troubles. Maybe even beginning to heal from the loss of his business.

"He is when he's in the wine room. He's happy with Dad and the boys. But with me? Not so much."

Mama frowned. "You're the boss. Trace might be owner. But you're the boss. Are you doing something he doesn't like?"

Only avoiding her dad. She wasn't about to tell her mother that. Or the fact that Trace had been correct. Here she had to stand tall, be the general manager she was trained to be. When she visited her parents in town, at their rental home, then she would be the mouse. Here, she had to be strong Marcia.

"No. He seems to like my work. It's my attitude." She took a quiet breath, then said, "I'm a bit cautious."

Her mother winced. "After Adam, who can blame you?"

Who indeed? Having a lover deceive her, steal from her family, shame her father was such a tangled mess that Trace was right. She was letting business and personal things overlap and now was the time to stand tall.

Like a good parent, Mama changed the subject. "Your dad wants a feast for lunch. He said there's a tourist break between one and two. If stragglers come in, one of the boys can handle them. But he wants to celebrate."

"Celebrate?" She gasped. "Trace buying this vineyard is his loss."

Her mother shrugged. "Maybe it's not so much a celebration as a welcome, then. No one welcomed Trace, and because it was our home, it's our duty."

She considered that and agreed. Maybe it was another step her father needed? A transition of a sort.

"Yes. Papa has been good to him, but no one officially welcomed him."

"See? Mama is always right."

That made her laugh. And feel good. Feel like herself. Even after her sort of scolding from Trace that morning, her sense of self blossomed. The vineyard felt more like the place she loved. Most of the tension went out of her shoulders. The impression that she was moving on filled her. Not in a bad way. In a good way.

The way a strong woman should embrace change.

But her father's celebration didn't go as planned. First, there was awkwardness when her dad took his seat at the head of the dining room table. Realizing that seat no longer belonged to him, he made a production number out of switching places with Trace, giving him the honor of sitting at the head of the table. Then he allowed Trace to pour everyone's wine, settling back with a fake smile.

Shame flitted through Marcia, but remembering Trace's orders from the morning, and the sense of her strength she'd felt about embracing this change, she kept her head high. Her spine straight.

A bus pulled in just as her dad lifted his glass to toast. Matteo pushed his chair back. "I'll get it."

"Good. Great," her dad said, at the same time that Trace said, "Thank you. I appreciate that."

As Matteo scrambled out of the room, her dad said, "Well, it seems nothing is on track today."

"Oh, I don't know," Trace said, lifting his glass. "We had a great morning. We sold lots of wine.

But more than that, I saw what a great man you are, Antonio." He lifted his glass a little higher. "To you, Antonio Giordano. A great man. Someone I hope will become a great friend."

Though Trace had intended his toast to be a salute to her dad, he didn't seem to realize he'd stolen her dad's moment. Antonio had wanted the opportunity to be gracious, to welcome Trace, but Trace had toasted him first.

After a stunned second of silence, Marcia said, "Hear. Hear."

Her mother and brother raised their glasses and her father smiled, accepting the salute, but Marcia saw the emptiness in his eyes.

Trace might want to fix things, but he'd just made things worse.

CHAPTER FIVE

ANTONIO'S SILENCE AT lunch was superseded only by his stony silence the rest of the afternoon. It hadn't taken Trace long to figure out that what had started as a way for Antonio's family to welcome him had become difficult for Antonio. He liked Trace, but he'd lost his life's work. That afternoon it was clear the old man was floundering for a place in the world.

After nine, when the sun had long ago set and the night sounds settled in, Antonio's truck chugged its way off Giordano Vineyards and Trace ambled into the house, exhausted. Not from tourists but from trying to make Antonio happy.

With a bottle of red taken from the wine room samples, he walked down the hall, to the kitchen and directly out to the dark patio.

He stopped when he saw Marcia at the table, staring out at the vineyards. He considered turning around but knew the click of the door closing behind him had alerted her to his presence.

He approached the table. "I see we had the same idea."

She smiled up at him. *"Si."* She rose. "I was just leaving."

He groaned. "Ah, come on. Don't do that. I have never felt more like an interloper than I did today with your dad."

"I thought you said you liked having him around."

He sucked in a breath. "My toast at lunch didn't exactly go over well."

"That's because you stepped on my dad's welcome-to-Tuscany toast to you. The lunch was supposed to be our welcome. You rolled right over my dad when he started to speak."

"Yeah. I figured that out. Your dad was low energy all afternoon." He took a seat at the table and poured wine into his glass, then offered it to Marcia. "Share?"

She hesitated but reached for the wine. "Sure." She took a sip and gave it back to him.

"Your brothers looked like they were walking on eggshells. They sold wine, but not like they had this morning." He sighed. "Your dad's behavior just reinforces everything my friends said last night. One difficult employee can make a mess of things for everyone."

He took a drink of wine and returned the glass to her.

"But if you ask him not to come anymore it

would break his heart. He can't be the object of any more gossip."

He closed his eyes. He really should not care about that. But he did. And not just because of her dad. Because of her. She'd been different that day. Stronger. Happier. How could he break their unspoken bargain that he'd keep her dad if she changed her behavior around him?

He couldn't.

"So, what we're saying is we have to wait for him to get back to himself."

"Maybe give him a few days?"

He sniffed. "In a few days, he could lose me thousands of dollars."

She caught his gaze, her dark eyes shiny in the moonlight. "You can afford it."

He laughed. "Yeah. I suppose."

She smiled. "Thank you."

His heart softened. Pleasing her felt like Christmas and Easter all rolled into one. And that was wrong too.

He quickly took the conversation back where it belonged. "I suppose I could help things along if I found a way to get him to cheer up."

She rose from her chair. "Good luck with that."

He sucked in a breath. Not only was she being flippant, but she was his general manager, supposed to help him figure things out.

She turned to leave, and he caught her hand, stopping her. When he rose to stand in front of her, he realized she was smiling, and her brown eyes sparkled.

"You're enjoying this."

"Maybe I like that the heat is off me for once. You said you wanted the tension eased between Papa and me. Knowing you're handling Papa is definitely easing mine."

He couldn't help it. He laughed. She had a great sense of humor, but more than that, he liked making her laugh about something that had just that morning had her nervous and on edge.

Still... It wasn't right. He was feeling things he wasn't allowed to feel, definitely mixing business with pleasure, when he knew better.

He shook his head. "I could virtually run our multibillion-dollar conglomerate in my sleep, and your simple family business is breaking all my rules, making me crazy."

She shrugged. Her lips turned up into a smile that stole his breath and made his blood race.

He still held her hand. They stood only a few inches apart. The full moon smiled down on them while the vineyard that was at the center of their problems rustled in the breeze.

But she was smiling. Amused by him.

The humor of it struck him and his own lips rose. "This is crazy."

"There's that word again. You use *crazy* a lot... especially about yourself."

She really was funny. Fun. He felt like he was

getting a glimpse of her as she really was, maybe as she had been before their employee embezzled.

With their gazes locked, everything inside him slowed to a crawl. Warmth suffused him, along with a yearning so pure he couldn't fight it. He inched closer. The connection between them rose, swelling around him, urging him even closer.

"I think I'm going to kiss you."

Her eyes didn't even flicker with surprise. And why would they? They'd been attracted since the second they'd laid eyes on each other.

"You shouldn't."

Her voice was a soft whisper that skipped along his spine, but she didn't move. Didn't step back. Held his gaze.

Expectantly.

The hum of whatever it was that buzzed between them drowned out his common sense and reasoning. Simple curiosity filled him, as desire surged in his blood and temptation promised fulfillment, pleasure enough to make it worth the risk.

He lowered his head and kissed her.

He meant it to be a brief kiss, but her lips were soft. And she'd been surprised enough that she'd gasped, opening her mouth the merest bit, enough to take the kiss from innocent to intimate without either of them trying.

He fell into the kiss like Alice down the rabbit hole. Her soft lips tempted him but also slowed him down to savor every movement, every sensation. Not merely her warm lips, but their height difference, the press of her breasts against his body.

His hands moved to her tiny waist, reminding him of her curves, and his nerve endings glittered and shimmied. She was physically perfect, but more than that, she was Marcia. Not a woman in a crowd. Not someone he chose because she didn't look like his ex. But someone he was coming to know. And like. And understand. Which made the kiss striking, important, breathtaking.

He sank even deeper. Thoughts disappeared. Desire lured him on to a place from which there'd be no return.

But she pulled away, bringing him out of his trance and back to the vineyard. The moon. The night sounds. The scent of the cooling earth.

For ten seconds she stood in front of him, her breathing ragged, her eyes confused. Then without a word, she turned and left him on the patio with a million stars winking overhead and one very disapproving moon.

Yeah, he got it.

All of it. Understanding her guilt over losing the vineyard, he should have realized she didn't need kisses or a baffled man acting out of character all over the place, making passes at her. She needed redemption. Peace. A second chance.

His brain stumbled over that realization. His breathing froze.

She *did* need redemption and a second chance.

Trying to solve her feud with her dad, his thoughts had always gone to removing her father from the vineyard. But what if Marcia was the one who should go?

The idea of losing her cut through him. With her kiss still on his lips, his heart stuttered at the notion that he'd never see her again.

But this wasn't his choice. Or at least it shouldn't be. He'd tied her to the vineyard with his need to smooth the transition from the Giordanos' hands to his. But what if that was the very worst thing for her?

After the spectacular kiss, Marcia carefully considered not joining Trace in the kitchen the next morning. No one had ever kissed her with such feeling. First, they'd laughed. Then he'd kissed her and that amazing connection she always felt around him lit like a firecracker, burned through the walls around her soul and awakened something in her.

A longing to be her total self again. Not merely businesswoman Marcia. But Marcia the woman. To find a partner. Someone to share her life with. To be in love.

Which was ridiculous. Wasn't going to happen. Everyone in her world knew of her sin, her mistake. She would always be the object of gossip in their little town, and even if they let her alone for a while, the gossip would resurrect every few years. Belittling her. She'd never be her total self again. Never be that overconfident woman again. Never risk falling in love. No matter how much he tempted her.

And he had tempted her.

It was one thing to be drawn into a kiss, lured by needs she hadn't felt in a year. It was quite another to have a sense of completion spin through her. The mastery of his kiss annihilated her senses, then brought them to stunning life again. The way he controlled it all spoke more of his need than words could have. She'd never experienced anything like that with Adam. And maybe that scared her the most. She'd trusted Adam with everything. Trace would demand even more. She knew it in the center of her being.

And a smart woman wouldn't let herself think about *that* too much. The intensity of what he made her feel might tempt her, but he was her boss. He owned her family home. He was strong, bold, remarkable. She was still figuring out how to right her life. They did not belong together.

That was the conclusion that had her turning away from him without a word the night before. There was nothing to be said when two people were so very, very wrong for each other.

She heard the rustling of pots and pans or maybe

the coffee maker, and her stomach growled. She was hungry and she needed coffee. Besides, she couldn't avoid him forever.

Particularly since being cool with him that morning could finish the job she'd started when she walked away from him after that spectacular kiss. They did not belong together. She would show him that.

She took a long, life-sustaining breath and walked into the kitchen. "Good morning."

His gaze rose and he gave her a quick once-over as if assessing her mood. "Good morning, yourself. What's on the agenda for the day?"

She hadn't expected him to jump right to business. But why not? She wanted to send a message. This was the perfect way to get things back to normal between them. Rather than apologize for kissing her, question her about why she'd left without a reaction, or kiss her again, he asked about her schedule. Making all those things moot.

Which was good. She should be grateful—

Still, after such a powerful kiss the night before, why *wasn't* he apologizing? The man worried about lawsuits over her cooking. Yet he'd kissed her? Why wasn't he worried that she'd sue him over that? Plus, if he'd decided he liked her enough to kiss her once… Why didn't he want to kiss her again?

She almost groaned. She had to stop thinking like this! She'd made up her mind. They were not right for each other! She should roll with this easy out he was giving them.

She pasted on her professional smile. "Actually, the vineyard is closed on Thursdays. You're free."

"I don't have time to be free!"

His voice was oddly desperate, and she frowned.

"The sales agreement says you can leave in a year. We extended that with a bet, but that doesn't preclude you from giving up when the amount of time in the sales agreement runs out." He paused and caught her gaze. His eyes shifted, changed from aggressive to soft and warm. "And you might want to leave sooner."

Ah, so he hadn't forgotten that kiss after all.

She took a breath, then another, not quite sure what to say. A romance between them might be foolish, but that didn't mean she hadn't liked the kiss. It had been an entire year since anyone had kissed her. A year since her heart rate had jumped and her bones had melted. A year since anyone had looked at her with interest, let alone acted on it.

He'd made her feel beautiful, desired. The part of her that always went after what she wanted swelled and nudged her to tell him that.

But that would be wrong. They were opposites. People in two different places in their lives. She couldn't fall for him. One of them would surely get hurt.

Finally, she settled on saying, "I'm fine." Something so neutral she let him know she wasn't offended, even as she soothed her aching heart by drawing on her strength of purpose. She would not willingly walk into a complicated situation again.

She reached for a mug and got some coffee, giving him time to process those few simple words, then changed the subject. "Do you want to go over the books today?"

"I went over the books before I bought the place."

She took a sip. "How about a tour through the grapes?"

He frowned suddenly. "I'm sorry. It just hit me that I'm stealing your day off." Taking in her jeans and T-shirt, he waved his hand. "Go do whatever it was you had planned to do today."

He might have tried to make it seem that the look he'd given her was neutral, but something sparked in his eyes. Something strong enough to make her think of that kiss again.

Luckily, her phone pinged with a text. "No. It's okay. If you want to work, we'll work." She pulled her phone from her jeans pocket and tapped the screen. "There *is* a lot for you to learn in a year. I'm happy to teach you."

He snorted. "Are you sure?"

"I'm sure." Seeing the text was from Janine, she took a breath before she tapped the phone to read it.

"I could probably find something else to do."
He rose and filled his coffee mug again.

She quickly scanned the text.

Hi. This is Janine's assistant, Carla. She wanted me to text you to let you know she got your message. But we have some sad news. Her mom's lung cancer is not responding to the experimental treatment her doctor had found. They've given her no more than a few months to live.

Marcia about dropped her phone. She knew how close Janine and her mother were. As close as she was to her own mother, she couldn't imagine the heartbreak of losing her.

She will get back to you as soon as she can, but right now she's only going into the office sporadically. She's focusing on her mom.

Marcia typed back.

As she should. Give her my love and tell her that if she needs anything, she should call me.

"Or maybe I *should* take a day off?"
She looked up at Trace. His pretty blue eyes behind the lenses of sexy glasses. His great hair. Those unexpected tattoos. He was a man who

kissed with real emotion. He didn't just go through the motions. He *kissed*.

He felt things. And no matter how much she tried to deny it, they had connected.

The need to tell him about Janine raced through her. Not the fact that it could take months before she'd have the money to buy him out, but that her friend was losing her mother. The sadness of it. The awful feeling that life changed too often and when you least needed or wanted it to.

She had the sense that he would understand. But she also recognized he was her competition. Janine had been Marcia's way out—a chance to repair her relationship with her father by giving back the vineyard she'd lost. Now, also, a chance to get away from this man who didn't merely tempt her physically. Something about him made her long to confide. And that was scary. Especially after falling for Adam had nearly ruined her life.

She could hope Janine went into the office looking for a few minutes of normal in a very dark situation and started the ball rolling on giving her the loan, but that was selfish.

She took a breath, shored up her emotions, quickly remembered Trace had said something about taking a day off and forced herself back into their conversation. "Do all-business bosses take a day off?"

Trace sat on one of the stools by the big island again. "I didn't used to." He glanced around. "But I wanted this experience to be different... So maybe I should shake things up? Take the day off?"

"Maybe?"

"Okay. I *probably* should."

She glanced down at her half-empty coffee cup. Becoming friends, getting to know each other, was an unintended consequence of living together, but God help her, she was curious. What kind of guy never took a break?

She turned to refill her cup, hoping to make her comment seem casual, offhand, even though her questions about him were mounting so high she could no longer contain them and had to have at least some answers. "You sound like you've never rested before."

"I took vacations." He sniffed a laugh. "I was actually here a few years ago. It's part of why I could so easily buy this place. I knew I loved Tuscany."

She sat beside him at the island. "Where else did you go?"

"Key West in Florida with Cade."

"One of your partners?"

"Yes. He loves to fish. Lots of charter boats in Key West. I also spent most Christmases on a tropical island. I'd work Christmas Day." He peeked over at her. "You have to have grocery stores open on Christmas Eve so people can get

last-minute ingredients for pies and baked ham.
I'd take care of Christmas Eve's accounting on
Christmas Day. Then I'd catch a flight or charter
a plane and go somewhere warm. Wyatt would
take over the day after Christmas. Then after a
few days, he'd be off, and Cade would step in."

"Seems like an efficient team."

Something flickered in his eyes. "We were."

"You miss them."

"Yes." He glanced at her again. "As soon as I
get furniture, they'll be visiting."

She was surprised at how much that pleased
her. She wanted to know about his friends. Who
were these people who called him Mr. Fix-It, yet
shared responsibilities like brothers? "That'll be
nice."

"You think so now. But they will razz the hell
out of you."

"Me?" She blanched, her own fears racing back,
though they were never far from her brain. "Because someone embezzled on my watch?"

He shook his head and laughed. "No, because
you're pretty and funny. You're clearly smart. You
said you went to school in the States. They'll like
that."

Her heart lifted a bit. "They'll tease me?"

"And love every second of it."

She would too. She would love to be around
people who would treat her normally. "They
sound like fun."

"They both have a wicked sense of humor."

And now she understood why he was the one who hired and fired employees. The other two were fun. He was the serious one, their counterbalance. "So, you became The Eliminator by default."

He laughed. "Yes and no. I have a more serious side than either one of those yo-yos."

Exactly what she'd thought. Her heart warmed, even though she knew it wasn't wise. Beneath that all-business exterior was a very nice guy. She'd gotten more than one glimpse of him. And she had the sense that no one ever did anything nice for him.

"We could go to Siena."

He peered at her over his coffee cup. "Excuse me?"

"Siena," she said, her confidence growing. "It's an interesting little city. Less crowded than Florence. It would be the perfect break for you."

She watched his face as he considered it and was surprised when his smile grew.

"I do need a day off."

He did. She could tell he did. But so did she. When she was with him, she forgot her past. Forgot to be careful because she'd made a horrible mistake. Some days she needed a break too. Taking him to Siena had the twofold effect of forgetting her troubles and helping him forget his.

"Do you like art?"

He laughed. "I like knowing things, being cultured."

She rose from her seat. "Then we're going to up your culture today."

He laughed again. "Okay."

Her heart fluttered. The joy of doing something for someone else filled her. Along with the freedom of forgetting everything and living in the moment. "Okay."

She frowned.

He shifted on his seat, getting more comfortable. "I'm not saying we trick your father. But once we investigate a few vineyards and pick the best two or three, the ones with the most potential, we could take him to those, telling him I'm thinking of buying a second and need his opinion."

"Then he would point out everything you'd need to do to get it up and running—"

"And hopefully see the opportunity himself. Even if he doesn't buy it, we'll start the wheels turning in that direction. Eventually, he'll see this is what he should do."

She snorted. "Not if I'm involved. As long as we keep me out of it, I think the idea has a chance."

"Look, I get that he's mad at you. Being general manager and giving an employee so much access without controls, the bottom-line fault does rest with you." He frowned. "Why weren't there checks and balances on that money?"

She took a breath. "Adam talked my father out of having them."

Trace blinked. "*Your father* actually gave him full control over the money from that first loan?"

"I don't think my dad realized that was what he was doing."

He waited a few seconds, probably trying to figure out her dad's rationale, and when he couldn't, he said, "What on earth did he think he was doing?"

CHAPTER SIX

"I CAN'T BELIEVE I'm on a bus." Trace glanced around at the passengers in the seats near theirs. Mostly tourists. "It was bad enough you forced me to get on a train, but the bus is like adding insult to injury."

She laughed. "You have to have a special permit to park in Siena. We didn't have one."

Her answer was matter-of-fact, simple. Nothing like the scenery around them. As they pulled into the bus station, he could see the buildings were a complicated collection of various kinds and periods of architecture.

But it was also breathtaking. He'd been to Italy. That's why buying a vineyard had been so appealing. But in this city, Siena, he felt like he was seeing more than tourist attractions. He was seeing the real Italy.

The bus let them off and Marcia pointed. "Let's walk this way."

They began to move, leaving behind tourists poring over maps and brochures, and the ambience of Siena hit him like a punch in the gut. Air rich with the scents of baked goods and pasta swirled around them in a soft breeze. Warm sun beat down on them. The sounds of laughter and delight flowed to them.

The place was old, crowded and filled with the kind of joy that was contagious.

"This is something."

"I'm surprised you didn't stop here on your trip to Italy a few years ago."

He laughed. "I'm guessing I was put off by needing to take a bus after a train."

She laughed too and, in a surprising move, slid her arm around his at the elbow. Keeping them close, he was sure, so they didn't get separated in the clusters of tourists. But being connected to her made him even happier than he already was.

"This is a place of history." She motioned around with her hand. "It was once bigger than Rome. We have art, architecture, culture."

He followed the movement of her hand, feeling so many things he wasn't sure he could define them. The city was gorgeous. The air vibrated with simple joy. But with Marcia's hand tucked at his elbow, he felt the weirdest kind of peace. He barely knew her. Sure, he'd kissed her. But, really, they'd been in each other's lives only a few days. Yet it felt so right to be with her. To enjoy this city with her.

"Your choice," she said, guiding him into Piazza del Campo. "We can get a quick lunch or sightsee, then eat."

"Let's walk some more." He pointed in front of them. "I'd like to see inside that cathedral."

As they approached it, he googled it on his phone and began to read. "'Siena Cathedral is a medieval church in Siena, Italy, dedicated as a Roman Catholic Marian church, and now named for the Assumption of Mary.'"

They walked inside. Silence and reverence surrounded them, but as they moved farther inside, the sounds of the tourists echoed in the high-ceilinged sections. They didn't talk as they looked at the magnificent arches, the white-and-black marble columns, the mosaics on the floors.

Just seeing the age of everything rendered him speechless.

It wasn't until they got outside that he spoke. "That was amazing." He shook his head. "You are so lucky to live so close to this much history."

"We know. You Americans are babies compared to us."

He peered around. "Yeah, our two hundred years probably seem like a drop in the bucket to most of you."

She laughed and the weird joy filled him again. Her skin was smooth and clear. Her nose pert. Her lips plump and, today, always lifted into a smile. But her eyes held the real temptation. Dark and teeming with emotion, they caught his gaze. Tempted him to linger. To connect.

For ten seconds, he fought the urge to slide his hand around the back of her neck and pull her close for a quick kiss. Only with great determination and the reminder that he wasn't the happy guy she was dealing with today did he keep himself from kissing her long and deep, enjoying the moment. Enjoying *her*. He couldn't draw her into feelings he wasn't sure of himself. Emotions so bold and spontaneous, they took him when he least expected.

But, oh, he wanted to.

They spent more time examining the Palazzo Pubblico and museums. Caught up in the beauty of the area and how easy it was to be with Marcia, he didn't realize the passage of time until she reminded him that they had better get lunch, which would now be an early dinner.

They decided on a restaurant near the tower and ate pasta with Bolognese sauce and roasted chicken.

As they walked out of the restaurant, Trace laughed. "I don't think I'm going to be able to eat again for a year."

She laughed too. "Good, because by the time we get home it will be too late to eat again."

He didn't know why everything she said made him feel light and airy. He would use the word *comfortable*, but it was more than that. She made him forget. His past. The weirdness at the vine-yard. Even the fact that he wasn't supposed to like her.

They took the bus to the train talking about what they'd seen, but when they got into the passenger car, silence reigned.

It wasn't strained, but that was the problem. He should be maintaining his distance with her. Instead, he felt like they'd been friends forever. And he shouldn't. He had too much of a past to think he could handle a future. He wasn't giving her back her vineyard. He intended to live at Giordano Vineyards. And just as he'd thought the night before, she should be moving on—

He couldn't fathom it. It might be the right thing for her, but it didn't feel right in general. He knew she needed a second chance. She needed to redeem herself. But in another city where no one would see? The people of her town wouldn't know?

Could her leaving actually be construed as running?

It could. But how could she stay at a vineyard—or in a town—where her sad, angry father reminded everyone of her mistakes?

Staring out the train window, watching the world go by, he saw a for-sale sign on the huge gates of a vineyard. A few miles down the tracks, he saw another.

He frowned. He would have never bought either one of those vineyards. Even from a distance it was clear they needed a lot of work. But he'd bet they'd be much cheaper than Giordano Vineyards had been—

They would be cheap. Probably less than half of what he'd paid for a vineyard that was up and running, making a profit—

His brain began humming.

He glanced at Marcia. Glanced back at the lush Tuscan landscape. Saw the third for-sale sign that whipped by as the train passed it. He thought about Antonio's anguish. His loss. The man was barely in his fifties. He could either let this loss define him or he could start again.

He almost laughed. The answer was so simple it was brilliant.

He faced Marcia. "I've been thinking about your dad."

She shifted to look at him. "Oh, yeah?"

"Yeah, and I think I've come up with an answer to the problem."

"You mean him not being cheerful with tourists?"

"Well, that and your family losing your vineyard."

She quirked an eyebrow.

Not sure if she was interested or perturbed, he plunged on. "If you take all the emotion out of your family's situation, your dad lost a business because he trusted an employee. If you're going to make a mistake, that's the best kind to make.

It proves you put yourself out there. And someone else actually did the deed that ruined you."

She snorted. "That's a funny way of looking at it."

"That's an objective way of looking at it. Business is supposed to be objective. Not emotional. Your dad made great wine, had enormous sales, grew healthy grapes. He did everything right but hire that guy... What was his name?"

"Adam."

"Adam. If he hadn't hired Adam, he'd still own Giordano Vineyards. It didn't change his ability to run a vineyard or his smarts about making wine. That one mistake shouldn't run him out of business. In fact, with his know-how and experience, he should get back on the horse."

She furrowed her brow. "We don't have horses."

"Not a real horse. It's an American expression. It means he should take the money he has left over from selling Giordano Vineyards and buy another."

She gasped. "He can't afford another vineyard!"

"Sure he can. Your dad had all kinds of equity in your business. He simply didn't have the cash for big monthly payments on millions of dollars in loans. But what if he didn't borrow any money? What if he bought something for cash?"

Marcia knew what Trace had paid for the business. The overage wasn't enough for what he was suggesting.

"If my calculations are correct, there still isn't enough left over to buy a thriving vineyard."

"No, but there is enough to buy one that needs work. Your dad has seed money. He has two strapping sons. Right now, they work in the wine-tasting room, but they are young enough and strong enough to do a good day's work."

The point of his idea finally breaking through, she sat up on her train seat.

"You agree with me, don't you?"

A little dazed, she gave herself a minute to let the fullness of the suggestion sink in and finally said, "Yes." She winced. "Sort of."

"No *sort of* about it. He comes to Giordano Vineyards every day because he's bored. He's bored because he needs a challenge. He has everything he needs to buy another vineyard—one he can develop again. He's just sulking."

"And mad at me."

"Yeah. No kidding. But he can't use that as an excuse. He should be saying, 'Lesson learned about trusting the wrong person,' and then jumping in to create competition for me."

She laughed and pulled her fingers through her long curls. "It makes perfect sense, but I don't think my dad will go for it."

"Then maybe we help him along?"

She sniffed. "It will be a cold day in hell before my dad listens to anything I suggest."

"So, we don't suggest. We lure."

She frowned.

He shifted on his seat, getting more comfortable. "I'm not saying we trick your father. But once we investigate a few vineyards and pick the best two or three, the ones with the most potential, we could take him to those, telling him I'm thinking of buying a second and need his opinion."

"Then he would point out everything you'd need to do to get it up and running—"

"And hopefully see the opportunity himself. Even if he doesn't buy it, we'll start the wheels turning in that direction. Eventually, he'll see this is what he should do."

She snorted. "Not if I'm involved. As long as we keep me out of it, I think the idea has a chance."

"Look, I get that he's mad at you. Being general manager and giving an employee so much access without controls, the bottom-line fault does rest with you." He frowned. "Why weren't there checks and balances on that money?"

She took a breath. "Adam talked my father out of having them."

Trace blinked. "*Your father* actually gave him full control over the money from that first loan?"

"I don't think my dad realized that was what he was doing."

He waited a few seconds, probably trying to figure out her dad's rationale, and when he couldn't, he said, "What on earth did he think he was doing?"

She took a breath. She hated telling him this, but she couldn't let her father take the blame for her mistake. "Showing his future son-in-law that he trusted him."

The space between them went silent for a second before Trace said, "His future son-in-law?" His eyes narrowed. "You're not telling me what I think you're telling me."

"Adam and I were engaged."

He gaped at her. "You hired someone you were engaged to?"

"No. We hired Adam when we knew we needed to expand. He was a specialist at getting loans at great rates and finding the subcontractors to do the work, all stuff outside the purview of the vineyard."

"He was your project manager?"

"Yes."

"No wonder your dad is so mad…and not at you. He's mad at himself."

She snorted. "Right."

"Oh, sweetie, if he were mad at you, this would be so much easier for him. But mad at himself? He's barely handling it." His voice filled with excitement. "That's the real reason we need to steer him in the direction of a new vineyard."

"For a second chance to prove himself—"

"No. A chance to prove himself *to himself*. Marcia, he's really hurting right now. I'm guessing his pride is stinging so badly he's driving himself nuts. Especially if the guy who took his money really did get off scot-free."

She sighed. "He's being pursued. But by the time we realized what had happened, he'd had eight hours' head start. No one using his name left the country, so we're thinking he has a new identity."

Trace shook his head. "You'll never find him."

"That's what the police say."

"That makes your dad's embarrassment all the worse."

She glanced down at her cell phone—always in her hand as she hoped for good news from Janine—then back at Trace. "If he really needs a second chance, my getting a loan and buying Giordano back for him might actually make things worse."

"Yes. If this is about his pride, your handing back the vineyard might send him into a tailspin. But if he has a chance to start over, that would be totally different."

Trace nudged her shoulder with his. "What do you say?"

With their gazes locked, she thought about that kiss. Warm. Melting. So emotional her heart fluttered just thinking about it. Was it such a good idea to get even more involved with a guy she was so attracted to?

They had a whole year to work together. If they found her dad a new vineyard, a project to help him redeem himself, there'd be no extension of her brothers' time at Giordano Vineyards. Her dad's visits would stop too. It would be her and Trace finding new employees, harvesting the grapes in the fall...doing all the work—

Together.

Her breath shivered at the thought. She knew everything there was to know about the vineyard. She wasn't afraid of that. But there would be no one else to teach him, no one to show him the ropes...except her. They'd spend days together. Just the two of them. Planning. Working. No interruptions from her family.

But she also realized that her dad needed another chance. And she did too. Starting over without her family, hiring new employees, training them, supervising grape harvest—she could do all of that in her sleep. And maybe working with Trace to reboot Giordano Vineyards was *her* second chance.

She got the feeling he already knew that and her respect for him jumped a hundred notches.

Maybe the thing she needed to focus on here was how much working with this very smart Mr. Fix-It would teach *her*.

"I'm in."

CHAPTER SEVEN

TRACE DIDN'T WASTE TIME. As soon as they finished their breakfast Friday morning, he went to the master suite and got his laptop. He pulled up the website of the real estate agency that had found him Giordano Vineyards and brought it to the kitchen. Sliding it to the island in front of her, he stood behind her as she flipped through the properties offered for sale.

"Wow, look at this one." She glanced behind her at Trace. "Why didn't you buy this one?"

It *was* grand. Acres and acres of land. A huge wine building. A villa fit for a king. But the villa sat in the far-left corner, close to the villa of the neighboring vineyard.

"I wanted privacy."

"Really?"

Wow, she smelled great. As if it wasn't difficult enough that visions of her laughing the day before kept rolling through his brain, now her scent teased him.

"Yes."

A strange feeling ruffled through him again when he added how attracted he was to her to how alone they'd be when her dad and brothers stopped coming over.

"You recognize that to make this work, I'll have to let your brothers out of their agreement to work through grape harvest."

"Yes. I figured that out. It's very generous of you."

"It also means you and I will have to work the wine room until I replace them."

She scrolled down the real estate agency's page. "I loved working there. While I was at university, before I transferred to a school in the States, I was head of that room when my dad was unavailable." She peeked over her shoulder at him again. "So much fun. Almost like playing."

He could picture it. Her in the white shirt and dark trousers. All that glorious black hair spilling around her. Smiling at tourists. Chitchatting about the area, the grapes, the process of making wine.

"In other words, you'll be fine with that."

She peeked back at him again. Her dark eyes soft and warm. "Yes. Thank you for letting my dad have my brothers to help him."

Her sincerity touched him more than a thousand sexy sparkles would have. He thought of her dad, the guy she so desperately wanted to help. And now he did too. Not just for Antonio, but for *her.* To help her get her life on track. To give her a second chance to prove herself. With her dad working his own vineyard, she could strut her stuff at Giordano.

"I couldn't enforce that clause in the agreement, knowing your dad needed them."

She laughed. "Where has The Eliminator gone?"

He shook his head. Where had The Eliminator gone?

Worry about the strength of his feelings for Marcia crept into his brain. Half concerned, half determined to help her, he fell to the seat beside hers and grabbed for the easy answer to defuse the conflicting feelings running through him. "I guess I really am more of a Mr. Fix-It."

She studied him for a second. "Something's happening with you."

He sniffed a laugh. "No kidding."

"Want to tell me?"

"Tell you what? That I took one look at you my first day here, knew you had troubles, pretty much decided I should fire you, then you tempted me with a challenge?"

She looked affronted. "You said you like a good challenge."

"I do."

"So that's normal."

"Not really, because I kept seeing your side of the story, got chummy with your dad, saw the rift between the two of you and realized I couldn't fix it short of getting rid of one of you."

Her head tilted. "And you found a way to do it nicely."

"Sure."

He was going way above and beyond his responsibilities, but he couldn't seem to stop himself. He knew it had more to do with liking Marcia than helping her dad, but if he admitted that, then he had to admit his feelings. That wouldn't be good for either him or Marcia—

Especially Marcia.

"It has to be the Mr. Fix-It in me. No other solution made sense until I came up with this."

She smiled and warmth careened through him. "Bet your friends had a field day with deciding to help my dad buy a vineyard."

The warmth grew until it tightened his chest and filled him with the weird sensation he hadn't felt since middle school when he got his first crush on a girl. But he was a player now. That's what his friends said. He didn't do relationships. He just had fun. He could not get involved with this woman.

He also knew that, like gossip, attractions could sometimes be killed with a good dose of reality. Bring the problem out in the open, see it for the preposterousness that it was and end it.

"I haven't had a chance to run this by them yet. Plus, my friends would be more interested in the fact that I like *you*. I've got to admit, it's given me some trouble."

She turned her stool to the left to look at him fully. She didn't play coy and act as if she hadn't noticed he was attracted to her. He'd kissed her. She knew.

"Try being the woman who was engaged to the man who embezzled from her family."

He hadn't forgotten that. He'd simply been so gobsmacked by it he'd never asked for more explanation. "I can't even imagine."

"I thought we were so in love. I made such a fool of myself." She pulled her fingers through her glorious hair. "We got an apartment in town. Were always at the tavern, playing darts, drinking wine, cuddling up to each other." She shook her head. "I thought I'd found my Romeo."

"Maybe you had? Maybe all that money with no controls simply tempted him too much."

She snorted. "He was the one who talked my dad into no controls, remember?"

He winced. So much for making things look less egregious. "Yeah."

"The fact that he could disappear so easily proves he'd been planning this for a long time." She drew a quick breath. "Now, I feel like an ass when I go into town, knowing people like Gina saw it all, saw how he snookered me." She took a breath. "You'd think I'd be wise enough never to be attracted to a man again."

His breath froze. She might not realize it, but she'd just admitted she was attracted to him too. Still, giving in to these wonderful feelings would only make her situation worse. "So, this is awkward for both of us?"

She laughed. "Yes. Awkward."

She caught his gaze and he saw the debate in her brain by the way her eyes darkened. For a good ten seconds he was sure she would change the subject. Instead, she said, "Awkward but also interesting."

His nerves exploded like little fireworks and he groaned. "Don't say that! I'm having enough trouble dealing with this. We don't need to add telling me you find our attraction interesting. I'll take that as a sign that you're interested in *me*."

"I am interested. You're gorgeous and usually nice."

He shook his head, afraid to answer, afraid he'd say something he'd regret or, worse, draw her in.

"You're also in control most of the time. Very manly. You're absolutely my equal." She smiled at him again. "All things *any* normal woman would be attracted to. Reminding myself of that keeps me from reacting or saying or doing something stupid. I tell myself 'of course you're attracted to him. Every woman in the world would be.'"

He wanted to argue that not every woman in the world would be attracted to him, but pride stopped his breathing until he saw her point. She was gorgeous. Of course he was attracted to her.

"So, those times when I want to kiss you, all I have to say is, 'Of course you want to kiss her. She's stunning and has beautiful hair.'" He paused to let himself run his fingers through the curls, which weren't corkscrew today. They were softer, some of them almost waves rather than curls. "Eyes that spark with fire one minute and fill with warmth the next."

"My eyes do that?"

"Yeah." He leaned closer. "It's why I kissed you. You'd never given even one overt indicator that you were attracted to me, but your eyes have this way of softening that somehow seems like an invitation."

Her lips slowly pulled up into a smile. "Been a long time since someone said anything that romantic to me."

"Well, they should." His hands were on her curls again. Soft, sensual, they tickled his fingers. The urge to kiss her slid through him. His instinct was to fight the sensation, but the curious look in her eyes had him rethinking that.

How had he thought getting their attraction out in the open would rob it of its power? Right now, he wanted to kiss her more than he wanted the vineyard—and *that* scared him silly. Get involved with another woman for real? Risk his heart? His sanity? Or wake up one morning and find her gone, his son a mere memory? His heart bleeding from loss?

He rose from his seat. "Tell you what. You go into the office and hunt for vineyards on that computer, and I'll do the same on this laptop. Anything that overlaps, we'll investigate."

She searched his eyes. Trace wasn't sure what she was looking for, but eventually she said, "Sounds good."

She slipped out of the kitchen, leaving him with a terrible feeling in the pit of his stomach. Longing mixing and mingling with fear. He reminded himself that his first marriage hadn't worked out, reminded himself that he'd lost a child. Told himself that Marcia was vulnerable. And a man who never slept more than two hours a night had to be vulnerable too. It wasn't wrong to be attracted to a woman. But letting that attraction drift over into something more emotional was.

He rifled through his soul to find the detached part of himself that could take everything he felt and snuff it out until he was totally empty.

Once he found it, he pulled the laptop closer and began searching for vineyards. But when he walked out to the patio in the middle of the night, unable to sleep, he thought of her. He knew she appreciated his plan to help her dad, but he also knew her attraction was as strong as his.

He told himself to forget that. But he couldn't. Thinking about her, remembering the feel of her hair skimming his fingers, remembering their kiss, her eyes, nudged a lot of bad memories aside.

Staring at the purple sky, he let the sweet thoughts of their kiss surround him, allowed himself the pleasure of remembering it until the sky began to lighten and he went upstairs again.

He didn't try to sleep. He hated the failure of sleep that wouldn't come. Instead, he went to the shower, then dressed for the day.

One of these nights he would sleep. He had to. But if sleep wouldn't take him, having the kiss of a beautiful woman to think about wasn't a bad way to pass the lonely hours.

The only worry was that all that time spent thinking about her might be dangerous. If he let his daydreams go too far, they would eventually edge over into reality.

The following night, when he found himself thinking about her kiss, he forced his thoughts back to finding a vineyard for her dad and his plans became more detailed. If his brain drifted back to Marcia a time or two over the next few days, he didn't worry. He'd think about her dad's new vineyard and be drawn away from thoughts of her. Work always could drown out the part of his brain that wanted too much. As long as he was busy, he was strong. Invincible.

And no longer thinking about his son. Not wondering if there had been something he could have done, something he should have seen the night his little boy had drifted to sleep and simply never woke up.

But soon thoughts of work mingled with thoughts of Marcia because she was part of the vineyard. And thoughts of Marcia tiptoed over into the way she felt in his arms, the glorious softness of her hair, and some nights he let himself go there.

He stayed away when she was in the house. No more dinners. No more sharing wine. But every day it got more and more difficult not to talk to her, and he told himself this was stupid.

They were two consenting adults who liked each other. Surely, they could work this out.

Thursday afternoon, they took the Maserati down five miles of winding roads to a vineyard where Trace's real estate agent would meet them. Marcia had tried to talk twice, but with wind whipping around them, she gave up and simply enjoyed the ride.

When they arrived at a property with big white iron gates, he rolled the car to an empty security station and hit a button.

"Hello?"

"Hello! Yes! This is Ruth Montgomery. Your real estate agent. I'll open the gate for you."

The old doors pulled apart slowly and Trace inched his car forward on a cobblestone driveway overgrown with grass and weeds. "Love the cobblestone. Needs some TLC though."

"Agreed," Marcia said. "You know, on the subject of work. I was thinking that maybe we should start scouting for people to replace my brothers right now...before they leave."

"Fresh air really does make you think, doesn't it?"

She laughed. Once she'd realized talking was pointless, the air that swirled around the convertible as he drove had made her feel fanciful and pretty, happy in a way she hadn't been in a long time. All because he'd said a few words and touched her hair as if it were spun gold, causing her heart to soften. Though he'd spent a week avoiding her, she'd still had to force her mind to stop thinking about him. Strategizing the impact his plan would have on Giordano Vineyards seemed to be the only way to do that.

"My major takeaway from your idea is that we have to do it right if we're going to do it. Not just set up my dad to be busy and happy again, but make sure your operation stays intact."

He grinned at her. "Because you like me."

Her already soft heart melted. A week apart had done nothing to change their attraction. The first time they were alone together, he flirted with her.

She knew it was wrong. That was why she wouldn't let herself dwell on his admission that he liked her. It was why she wouldn't let herself go over and over the memory of how he'd touched her hair...so reverently, as if he couldn't stop himself.

"I didn't say I liked you. I said you were interesting."

He got out of the car. "Same thing."

"Yes, well, it seems to me that your happiness about that means you like me too."

He closed the door. "Yeah, but you like me enough that you thought you had to stay away from me for a whole week."

She could have told him it hadn't helped. Their curiosity about each other still raged. But she hadn't been the one avoiding him.

"I didn't stay away. *You* stayed away."

He looked at her over the car roof. "And it bothered you, didn't it?"

She stared at him. How was she supposed to answer that?

The villa door opened. Ruth walked out. "Good afternoon!"

A little breathless and extremely confused, Marcia closed her car door and walked around his sleek red vehicle toward the villa, toward Trace.

Her breath fluttered again when he put his hand on the small of her back to guide her to Ruth.

"Good afternoon." He shook Ruth's hand. Glancing at the overgrown trees, he said, "Some of this is nice."

Ruth winced. "Granted, it needs work."

Relieved for the distraction of the vineyard, Marcia looked around in dismay. "A lot of work."

They toured the villa and winemaking facility and would have headed out to the grapes, but Trace shook his head. "We'll keep this on the list in case nothing else pops, but I think there's too much work here."

Ruth smiled. "Okay. On to vineyard number two."

They drove a short distance to the second vineyard, but when Ruth told them the price, Marcia said, "No. That's too far over budget."

"But less work," Ruth reminded her.

Trace said, "Doesn't matter. We're sticking to the budget."

Vineyard three already had an offer. Ruth turned to Marcia. "Your father would have to beat that."

Once again, Trace said, "No."

The fourth was better. "Interesting," Trace said. Then he glanced at her and smiled.

Her breath caught when she realized he was using her own word to covertly flirt with her. She began to wonder if he'd stayed away from her all week because he knew this would happen. The last time they were together he'd flirted. And when they finally spent time together again, he flirted again. Almost as if he recognized he couldn't resist her.

"...but this vineyard would take us over budget too."

Ruth pulled out her phone. "Want to give me some specifics so I can get you closer to what you need?"

He shrugged. "We'll know it when we see it."

Having already locked the villa, Ruth left them with a big smile and a promise to find a few more vineyards to see the following Thursday.

They were silent in the car. With the Maserati's top down, it was a sort of safe zone because they couldn't talk. Couldn't flirt. Unfortunately, that didn't mean her mind didn't drift. She thought of their return to Giordano Vineyards and tried to decide if she should run into the house and to her room as soon as he stopped the car, or if she should continue the flirting game he'd started... see what would happen.

But Trace pulled into the parking lot of the first restaurant they found. They'd had breakfast, but no lunch, and the sun had already begun to set.

"I'm starving."

She sighed. "Me too."

"So, this is good?"

"This is good." She wasn't really 100 percent sure of that, but driving another hour with both of them hungry seemed idiotic.

Without a word, they walked into a cozy space where the hostess led them to a table in the back. She lit the candle. "Enjoy your dinner."

Trace looked around. "Why are Italian restaurants always so romantic?"

Maybe because he was in that mood? And that's why he'd flirted with her?

Not risking the conversation that observation would start, she said, "Has to be the candle."

He laughed. "Everything is kind of cozy."

Too cozy.

"Maybe we should talk about the vineyards we saw today."

"Good idea." He smiled and her heart lurched. He had the prettiest smile. It lit his blue eyes and transformed his entire face.

By the time their food arrived, they had exhausted the topic of the new vineyard. Awkward silence stretched between them. Soon questions about him popped into her mind.

She picked up her wineglass and swirled the red liquid. "You know, it just dawned on me that you know everything about my past, and I know very little about yours."

He gaped at her. "Are you kidding? You know where I went to school. You know about the business my friends and I sold. Hell, you know about my friends."

"You're saying you've told me more than you tell most people."

"Yes!"

She put her elbow on the table and her chin on

her closed fist. "Interesting that you've never told me anything about your relationships."

"That's because I don't have relationships."

She found that hard to believe and snickered. "You never have sex?"

He laughed. "I have girlfriends, but not relationships."

Her brow wrinkled.

He sighed. "Look, I don't do relationships because I had some really awful things happen in my past."

"That part I guessed." She waited for him to elaborate. When he didn't, she groaned. "Come on. I didn't have to tell you I was engaged to Adam, but I did."

He took a drink of wine. A few seconds passed. Then he pulled in a breath. "I could buffalo you by saying that when my friends visit, they'll spill the beans. So, I might as well tell you. But the truth is, you're curious because there's something between us, and telling you is fair."

It shouldn't surprise her that he'd admit there was something between them. He'd been pointing that out to her all day. But for it to be a reason for him to tell her his past? The attraction had to be more serious for him than she'd thought.

Her chest tightened, even as her curiosity piqued. Worried he'd back out before he told her anything significant, she swirled her wine in her glass again, pretending it was no big deal. "So, tell me this mysterious past you're so sure your friends will spill."

He sucked in another breath. "I was married."

She smiled and nodded. A really bad marriage explained why he would be gun-shy about relationships. But there was more. She could see it in the sadness in his blue eyes.

Finally, he said, "We had a son and he died."

The words came out in a rush, as if he was afraid that if he didn't say them quickly, he wouldn't say them at all.

Her eyes widened in surprise and horror. "Oh, my God. I'm so sorry."

He looked down at the table. "Please. You don't have to say that. I don't want sympathy."

"It's not sympathy to say that your loss was horrendous."

"You don't know the half of it. My wife's parents hated me. When our son died and she left, I knew they'd tugged her away or she hadn't really loved me in the first place. I was eighteen. I made the funeral arrangements alone. I had to talk to the coroner alone and agree to an autopsy because he died of sudden infant death syndrome." He shook his head. "One day I had everything I wanted. The next it was gone. As if all the good stuff I'd had was a dream and I woke up."

Shock and sadness poured through her. "I'm so sorry."

He leaned back. "No sympathy, remember?"

She did. But how could she feel nothing?

A few seconds went by in silence as he stared at his wine, but the difficulty of his past made it all the more important that he'd told her.

"Thank you."

He looked across the table at her. "For sharing that?" He tossed his napkin beside his plate. "I don't normally tell people. But like I said, what's happening between us is tempting and you shouldn't be tempted by me. Even if I can't resist you, you should resist me. I'm not the kind of guy you're looking for. I'm bitter about some things. Angry about others. And never going to have another serious relationship."

The sadness that coursed through her shattered her heart. For a few minutes, he seemed different. Older. As bitter as he'd told her he was.

While she was still reeling, he led them back into the discussion of what her dad would need in a new business, but unwanted pictures formed in her brain. She could see Trace as a father, loving a little boy he'd bring up to be as smart and confident as he was. She could picture him loving a woman so much that her walking away had devastated him.

Which was why he didn't take much time off. Why he needed to work. Even why the problem of her dad had lured him in. It was a distraction.

By the time they were finished eating, he was back to being himself. He'd encouraged her to talk about winemaking and growing grapes and analyzed everything she'd said. Until he not only seemed to have forgotten their discussion of his past, but they also had a comprehensive list to give to Ruth of what her dad would need in a new vineyard.

"This will help her," Trace said as they walked to his little red car.

"Agreed."

They slid inside. Trace revved the engine and soon they were back on the winding Tuscan road that would take them home.

As always, the wind kept them silent during the ride. Her nerve endings settled. Her heart found substance again, but the oddest emotion filled it. She absolutely did not feel sorry for him, but everything about him finally made sense. Along with that understanding came an enormous respect for him.

And new questions. He didn't have to tell her about his son. He could have told her about his ex-wife and left it at that. He'd told her so she really could know him. All of him. The truth of his pain. But she wasn't entirely sure he realized that. Or how telling it meant that he'd confided in her.

She didn't wait for Trace to open her car door. When he got out, she did too, and they walked to the villa door. He pressed the buttons on the keypad to disable the alarm and let them into the house. The nearly empty foyer greeted them. The sounds of silence surrounded them.

He smiled at her. "Shall we say good-night now and be awkward walking up the stairs together to our rooms?"

She laughed, telling herself that was not flirting. That was Trace being Trace. Seeing a problem and fixing it. He knew the things he'd told her could make their next few days together uncomfortable. He was facing it head-on.

"No." She started up the stairs. "Let's think about something to talk about that doesn't involve the vineyard or my dad. Then we can say goodnight at my room, and you can move on."

Behind her on the steps, he was quiet. Then he suddenly said, "It seems wrong."

"What? The vineyard list?"

"No. Us not having anything to talk about." He paused a second. Then he said, "You can be chatty."

She laughed. "Right. I'm the one who does all the talking."

"I like when you talk. When you tell me things. I loved seeing Siena and you telling me how to make wine. But most of all, I liked figuring out your dad's mess with you."

She heard the longing in his voice and felt the pull. The delicious temptation of a man realizing how much he liked her and how well they fit. A man who'd suffered a tragedy a million times worse than her own. A man who'd vowed never to get involved but couldn't seem to help himself. Because there really was something between them.

"Stop flirting."

"That wasn't flirting." He laughed. "That was me being honest."

"I like when you're honest."

"Maybe it's another thing we have in common. I'm not a fan of insinuation or guessing."

His easy answer seemed to break another barrier. The more they talked, the closer they got. Something neither of them wanted. He was wounded. She'd been deceived. Even if they were willing to risk it, a relationship between them would be difficult.

"We can always go back to talking about vineyards."

"I don't know how many times I can say those white gates needed painting without boring you."

Pleasure came before she could stop it. The deep, empty place inside her filled to overflowing and her laugh echoed down the hall. "Boring me is better than me wondering if you're staring at my butt."

"I hate to tell you this, but I stare at your butt every time I get a chance."

Oh, Lord. He probably believed telling her about his past was enough to stop her attraction. But if he kept saying things like that, she'd be putty in his hands. Those offhand comments made her feel whole, normal. And she wasn't. She'd been preyed upon, used, had a father who'd lost everything because of her.

And Trace wasn't any better. He'd lost a marriage. A child. He'd admitted to being bitter, angry.

They were the worst possible combination.

"Where is the guy who was worried that I'd sue him if he asked me to cook?"

"He got a good look at his bank account and realized he could afford a suit if you decided to go that route." They stopped at her door. "But you won't. Because this is consensual."

Before she could reply, he lowered his head and kissed her. Warm and sweet, his mouth moved over hers. For ten seconds, he weakened her knees and drew her to a place of complete oblivion.

Then he broke the kiss and smiled down at her. "Right?"

Her head spun. "Right, what?"

"This is consensual."

Once again, he didn't give her time to answer. He kissed her. His lips danced over hers until her breathing shivered in and out of her chest and her arms moved to his shoulders. Her fingers tunneled into the hair at his nape.

His hands slid from her back to her waist and settled there to nudge her closer. She went willingly. Longing opened her heart, then her soul. The strangest thought blossomed. What if two wounded people weren't the worst combination but the best? What if her feelings for him helped him…and his feelings for her helped her?

He deepened the kiss and her thoughts spun away until only feelings remained. His hands skimmed her back, sending tingles shimmying through her as they slid to her butt and back up again.

She put her hands on his cheeks, desperately taking control of the kiss, fearing he would end it. Instead, he stepped closer, pressing against her. Her pulse scrambling, their mouths meeting and withdrawing, tongues twining, she forgot her good common sense and threw herself into the kiss.

It was Trace who eventually backed away.

She stared at him, realizing she'd lost herself, forgotten her mistakes, forgotten those lessons, forgotten *his* pain, *his* misery, forgotten she had to work with him for an entire year.

She shook her head, not sure if it was to pull herself back to reality or if she'd done it to try to rattle some sense into her brain.

His kisses might lure her into believing they weren't the worst possible combination but the best. But she'd have slept with him if they'd kept going, and that was not something a smart woman jumped into without thought.

She turned and opened her bedroom door. "Good night, Trace."

She didn't wait for his answering goodbye. She stepped into her room and closed the door.

CHAPTER EIGHT

TRACE STARED AT her door for a full minute before he turned and walked down the hall to his room. The day had been long, peppered with work, good conversation and a kind of relaxation he hadn't experienced in years.

Most of their time together he'd told himself he felt better—felt good about himself—because he and Marcia were working toward finding her dad a new vineyard, a new life. Fixing things always gave him a boost. Good deeds added to that. That was why his chest filled with air and his thoughts didn't scatter. He kept his focus.

Then she'd asked him about his life, and he'd told her. Partially to be fair to her, but to remind himself that he didn't get involved with women beyond friendship and good times. He thought his confessions would nip their attraction in the bud.

They hadn't. The temptation to kiss her at her door had been four times as strong. The need to hold her had rattled through him, pushed him when he might have stood firm. The longing to forget everything had sent him over the top and he'd followed instincts he'd been fighting for a long, difficult week.

And it had been glorious.

Luckily, she'd left him standing in the hallway. He might be confused. He might even be confusing her. But eventually she'd come to her senses and had backed off. Exactly what should happen.

He'd told her he would never have another real relationship.

She'd responded like the smart woman that she was.

They could get past a few lush, primal kisses.

He walked into his bedroom. Ordinary, but squeaky clean, the master suite was obviously the former resting place of a husband and wife—

The thought sharpened his nerve endings. Memories of being a husband poured through him and he remembered being married, remembered how Skylar had loved him. How happy they'd been. How being a husband had been an odd combination of responsibility and joy.

Being a dad had been a stronger version of that. Every day after Joshua's birth, he had worked two jobs to earn enough money to support his little family and then come home to their tiny apartment, where happiness had filled his soul.

He glanced around, realized the homeyness of the Giordanos' bedroom was playing a part in bringing back his memories, and knew that once they found Antonio a vineyard, his next project had to be redecorating.

He almost grabbed the homeyness of the villa as his excuse for being overwhelmingly attracted to Marcia, but he knew that wasn't true. He genuinely liked her. She was gorgeous, smart, funny.

Wanting her had nothing to do with the vineyard.

But her longing made the need irresistible. He saw it in her eyes. Every time before he kissed her, they sharpened with desire, but also softened with a yearning to be happy. After a year of her dad's anger, the town's mocking and her own self-recrimination, she needed a little fun, and he was sure that was what tempted him the most.

He liked making her happy, making her laugh.

He dressed in sweatpants and a T-shirt and sneaked out of the bedroom that fueled memories he had to keep at bay. His phone in his pocket, he slid silently through the villa and out to the patio. For hours, he read news on his phone until his eyes drooped enough that sleep might not be far behind.

Returning to the house, he walked past Marcia's door without as much as a glance and dropped face-first on top of the covers on his bed. Sleep took him for a glorious hour and twenty minutes, but when his eyes opened again, the memories popped into his brain, along with the questions that always joined them.

Had he done enough?

Had he missed something the night Joshua died?

How much did Skylar blame him?

Was that why she'd left?

And *that* was why he couldn't get involved with Marcia.

A man who hadn't worked out his past couldn't create a future.

At lunchtime, Marcia waited until she saw her dad and brother Matteo leave the kitchen before she scooted across the parking lot to the villa for a sandwich. She was just about through eating when Trace and Roberto walked in.

Her eyes met Trace's.

The memory of his kisses the night before tightened her chest and sent shivers through her. The honest way he'd told her about his past and then held the odd conversation as they walked up the stairs had connected them. Again. Every time they were bare-bones honest, they seemed to get closer.

And that petrified her. She wanted something to happen between them. Wanted it so badly now that it almost seemed inevitable, but what if she got hurt again? He said he'd never have another real relationship. What if being with him made a fool of her again?

Worse, what if she somehow hurt him? A man already bowled over by sadness and incomprehensible loss didn't need a confused woman pining after him.

She picked up the remains of her sandwich and headed for the door. "Time for me to get back to work. You guys can have the kitchen."

She didn't wait for their goodbyes, just bolted.

But she couldn't avoid Trace that night. When she realized that, she decided to act as if nothing was different between them. He might have kissed her, but she'd been smart enough to back off. He'd told her the truth, warned her off, and she wasn't a silly girl with stars in her eyes, thinking love would conquer their problems. She'd backed off. She'd done the right thing. She could trust herself.

Taking some leftover pasta to the patio table where Trace sat eating a big salad, she said, "We never did talk about replacing my brothers."

He drew in a long breath. "I know. I watched them today, doing their thing, wondering how on earth I can replace that."

Grateful he was acting as normal with her as she was trying to be with him, she laughed. "They are good. But there are lots of other guys around who will be every bit as flirtatious and fun."

"That's great because I'm banking on your brothers helping to turn your dad's new vineyard into a gold mine." He set his fork down. "Speaking of which, Ruth has three properties scheduled for us to see on Thursday."

"She certainly doesn't let any grass grow under her feet."

"No matter which one your dad chooses, her commission will be hefty. I think she wants to be sure she doesn't lose us to another agency."

"Smart."

"Yes. She is."

He grabbed his fork again and continued eating. Marcia dug into her pasta. Normal conversation had calmed the space between them. But as they ate in amicable silence, the night sounds settled in. The sky darkened. The moon rose. The romance of the vineyard began to fill her.

She squeezed her eyes shut to get her bearings, but when she opened them again, she saw Trace and remembered his story. He'd been married too young to really understand all that he'd committed to and he'd lost his son.

Lost his son.

Her heart ached for him. She imagined he could have gotten over the end of his marriage if he hadn't lost a child. She didn't know much about how his son had died. He'd mentioned sudden infant death syndrome, but was there more?

For twenty seconds, she longed to ask for details, but as she tried to skew up her courage, she saw the fatigue in his eyes.

The sorrow.

That unfathomable emptiness. Something she couldn't pretend to understand.

She collected her dish and fork. "Good night. I'll see you in the morning."

He peeked up at her, over his glasses. "Good night."

Her heart fluttered. He was without a doubt one of the most attractive men she had ever met. The thought alone made her race to the door, but in the kitchen she stopped.

She absolutely could not deny her feelings for him. But suddenly instead of being afraid for herself, afraid of being hurt and damaging her reputation even more, she felt his loneliness. She felt his pain. But most of all she felt his need. And knew with absolute certainty that she was approaching this all wrong.

Fate might seem to have brought them together when they weren't a good match. But what if the truth was they were a match, just not a forever match?

Knowing him, working with him, trusting him had already brought her a long way toward healing.

Maybe it was time she helped him?

They might not be a forever couple. But maybe they were the right two people to help each other get to the next step of their lives?

Dinner had gone so poorly that Trace stayed outside longer than usual. Marcia had been normal one second, nervous the next. It was all he could do to get them through the meal.

When he was sure she was settled in her room, he walked to his, going through the same routine as the night before and returning to the patio once again.

He considered getting a bottle of wine but decided against it. He'd had his years of hard drinking. They'd only given him hangovers, hadn't soothed his mind. He watched the moon for a while, then clicked the app on his phone that brought his book on screen. He loved mysteries. He loved thrillers. With electronic books, he could have hundreds at his disposal in seconds.

He read until the sky became a red swatch. Realizing the sun was about to rise, he retreated to his room and slept at least an hour.

Knowing that was as good as he would get, he changed into his work clothes—black trousers and white shirt to match the crew—and went to the kitchen for coffee. Hungrier this morning, he made himself eggs and toast.

He was giving the eggs a final flip when Marcia walked in.

She stopped abruptly and her eyes widened.

With fear or surprise, Trace couldn't tell. But he had felt the awkwardness when she'd left for her room the night before. One minute he thought being with him scared her silly, the next he'd sensed their connection. The longer they sat together, the more comfortable they got. Even if they didn't want it, something drew them together.

They could avoid it, as she had the night before by leaving before things got too comfortable. But they still had to work together. He had to find the sweet spot where they could be good coworkers without tripping over into their attraction—

Without him kissing her.

Technically, this was all his fault.

He nudged his head toward his fried eggs. "Want these?"

She licked her lips. Part of him stared at that. She had thick, wonderful lips on a skilled mouth made for kissing.

The other part focused on her hesitation, the way she was nervous around him.

He shrugged. "I don't usually eat breakfast, but I'm hungry today. I only had salad last night."

"I'm hungry too." She'd finally spoken. Her voice hadn't shivered. She hadn't avoided his eyes.

"You take these, and I'll make myself two more."

"I couldn't!"

"Why not? We're partners in crime."

Her face scrunched. "Partners in crime?"

"Getting a vineyard for your dad? Already deciding your brothers' fate? We're like two evil geniuses."

She laughed.

"If you can't share eggs with a partner in crime, who can you share eggs with?"

She laughed again.

He held up the plate. "Come on. Take them before they get cold."

She reached for the eggs. "They smell wonderful."

"As I recall, you only had a little bowl of pasta last night."

"True."

"Which means, we either have to eat bigger dinners or plan to eat breakfast every day."

"Good point."

He nudged his head toward the toaster on the back counter. "There's toast too."

She found utensils and took her eggs and toast to the island. He made himself two eggs and more toast and sat beside her.

Tension wedged between them, but she smiled at him. "What's on your agenda today?"

"Working in the wine room. I'm finally making the connection that understanding what people want is the key to a good product."

She laughed. "No kidding."

He waved his hand in dismissal. "It's neither as simple nor as trite as you're trying to make it."

She smiled at him. "Sure it is."

Something woke inside him. That urge again to run his fingers through her hair. Brush a light kiss across her mouth.

He quickly looked away, but she slid her hand on top of his where it lay by his plate.

"Don't sell yourself short."

The need became a tightening. Not just in his chest, but all his muscles. Almost as if his body was resisting her compliment.

"I don't. Not often. But when I start something new, I realize I have a lot to learn."

She smiled again, holding his gaze. The connection surged between them. Everything he felt for her whooshed through his blood. He'd never experienced this kind of attraction for a woman before.

He bounced off his seat. "I've gotta go to work."

"Okay." When he reached for his plate, she caught his hand and squeezed. "Go ahead. I'll take care of this."

His breath shimmied. Every time she touched him, his entire body burst into flames. He raced out to the wine-tasting bars and tried not to watch her office door that morning, but it was no use. She'd been so different at breakfast—so open— that confusion took all his brainpower.

That afternoon, he noticed her retreating to the villa long before tourists had stopped arriving. About twenty minutes later, she walked out the front door, got into her car and left.

His heart dropped. Did he make her so nervous that she was leaving—?

To eat in town?

No. She would not eat in town. She might take a drive to avoid him—

But he had not made her nervous that morning. If

anything, she'd been oddly calm. She'd spoken naturally. Touched his hand. *Squeezed* his hand once.

If she'd left, it wasn't because she was angry with him.

So, what was it?

An hour later, she returned with four bags of groceries.

He froze. She'd gone shopping?

She'd only gone shopping.

The relief was so intense, he laughed. Shame on him for making a big deal out of nothing.

Antonio said, "That's right! Laugh! We have a great crowd tonight."

"Actually, Antonio, I'm kind of tired. I think I'll go in for the night and let you handle this."

He straightened with pride. "Absolutely."

After saying good-night to Matteo and Roberto, he headed for the house. He didn't shower. Didn't change. Just marched to the kitchen, where Marcia was putting away her purchases.

He had absolutely no idea what he was doing. Mostly because she'd changed the game that morning and he couldn't figure out why. "I can pay for those."

She shook her head. "No. You bought last time."

He frowned. "I'm the boss. I own the house. Food is my responsibility."

She glanced over, smiled. "No. You said we were partners in crime. As a partner, I can buy food once in a while."

He could drown in her eyes. He could drown in her, lose his troubles, live in the moment—

He sucked in a breath. Thoughts like that weren't helping anything. "Okay."

He walked to the grocery bags. Peering inside, he paused, then laughed. "Your mother's pasta."

"I called her this afternoon. I told her I'd be making a grocery run. Since we're also feeding my father and two hungry brothers, she suggested I stop by for a few bags."

He looked up and saw Marcia smiling at him. Temptation rumbled through him.

"Which would you like tonight? Spaghetti or tortellini?"

He suddenly realized she'd done this to surprise him. Not because she owed him but because she liked him. The possibility made his soul do a cartwheel. He'd warned her off, told her his awful past, but she hadn't reacted with sorrow or pity. She'd gotten him some of her mother's pasta.

Such a normal, easy, wonderful thing. "Can I help with anything?"

"Not tonight." She pointed at the door. "Go get your shower. Take a break."

Her brown eyes sparked with mischief, enhancing the beauty of her delicate features. Softness and femininity surrounded her, as if the shift from the office to their home had somehow made her more womanly.

His chest froze even as his blood turned to molten lava. He had to stop thinking like that or he'd find himself kissing her again. So, she'd done a nice thing for him? She was a nice person. It was not a big deal.

He left the kitchen, went to his room, got a shower and put on comfortable shorts and a T-shirt before he walked out to the patio, where a bowl of pasta sat on the table, along with a bottle of wine. She lit a fat candle.

Confusion rippled through him as he walked up to the table. She'd also changed into a pretty pink dress. "This is nice."

She smiled again. "Thanks."

The sound of her dad's old truck leaving made him realize how alone they were. They'd been alone every other night. But she was different today. Confusing him.

He pulled out her chair, then his. The pool sparkled in the moonlight. Only the candle lit their dinner space.

When he tasted the pasta with homemade sauce, hunger obliterated all thought. He ate four bites before he glanced over at her.

"This is fabulous. Thank you."

Her warm smile appeared slowly. "You're welcome." She picked up her fork and joined him in eating the pasta while drinking Giordano Vineyards' wine.

She asked about his day and he asked about hers, working to keep the conversation neutral.

Soon they were sipping more wine than taking bites of pasta and eventually both pushed away their plate.

The flame of the candle danced in a light breeze, but it wouldn't have mattered if it extinguished. Moonlight lit the patio, the pool, the vineyards beyond.

Peace settled over him.

He drew a breath, then another. This was why he'd bought this vineyard, but he also liked Marcia. Meeting her, getting to know her, had been a delightful bonus. She set her hand on top of his again and he stared at it for a second as desire shimmered through him. He glanced around the dark patio, looked at the candle, frowned at his empty pasta plate.

She'd really gone out of her way to make this night special—

Was she seducing him?

Nah. Couldn't be. The things she'd done were too ordinary. Plus, Marcia was kind. Generous. Preparing this dinner could be construed as nothing more than Marcia being kind to him—

But she was also attracted to him. And after the way he'd kissed her, she had to know he wanted her. Though putting her hand on his seemed innocent, for someone like Marcia it might actually be a big deal.

A sign. A *move*.

Meaning the next move was his.

He took a breath. There was only one way to find out.

"You look beautiful tonight."

With her untamed hair flowing around her like a black cloud and the straps of her little sundress skimming her shoulders, she looked like a goddess.

"Thank you."

"Had I known we were dressing for dinner, I'd have worn something better than shorts."

She braced her elbow on the table and leaned in toward him. "I like you in shorts. You look comfortable." She smiled. "Happy."

"You make me happy." He said the words before he had time to really think them through, but he realized he wouldn't take them back. This was Marcia. Special. Fun. Wonderful. And if she wanted to take what they had and run with it, he wanted that too. Telling her about his marriage, he'd laid to rest any unrealistic expectations. If she was leading them where he suspected she was leading them, it was with everyone's eyes wide open.

He reached over and took her hand. "You make me *very* happy."

She smiled at him. Moonlight winked at him off the water in the pool. The scent of the rich earth wafted around them.

But the area was silent. There wasn't anyone around for miles.

They could take forever being polite and kind, dancing around what they wanted. Or he could simply take them where they wanted to be without all the hassle and confusion.

He pushed back his chair, rose, kicked off his shoes, scooped her up off her seat, turned and jumped into the pool.

She squealed through a bubbly laugh. "What are you doing?"

He eased her out of his arms but kept his hold on her hands as she moved through the water. "I'm not sure. Stop me."

"Stop you?"

"Or don't."

He leaned over and kissed her. When he pulled back, he removed his glasses and set them on the edge of the pool before he yanked his wet shirt over his head and tossed it to the stone patio. "There's still time to back out. My shorts are next, then your dress."

Her eyes bulged. "What?"

"Say the word and I stop."

He waited, standing in chest-deep water with her before him. The choice in her hands.

"Things felt different between us today." He reached over and lifted her chin. "You made them feel different."

"Si."

"Because?"

"Because I like you and maybe I think I finally

realized that some things aren't meant to last forever."

He inclined his head. "Maybe."

"Doesn't make them any less real or any less important." Her eyes softened. "They are what they are."

She leaned forward and kissed him, resting her hands on his chest.

He let her lead, and when she finally broke the kiss, their eyes met again. He skimmed the lightweight dress over her head, tossing it over to his shirt.

She stood before him in only panties the same pale pink of her dress. He hadn't realized she was braless.

"Wow." He paused only a second before he said, "There's still time to change your mind."

She laughed. "No. We both want this. We're two adults who were lucky to find each other. We may not have a future, but we do have now."

He totally understood. It was how he lived his entire life. Forget the past. Don't think about the future. Just take now.

His hands on her elbows, he pulled her to him for a kiss, letting her breasts bump his chest as they floated in the warm pool water.

Everything inside him began to hum. With one smooth move, he got rid of his shorts and eased her against him again. Long and deep, their kisses fueled the fire as he let his hands roam her curves.

He broke the kiss and lowered his head to her breast. At the first touch of his lips to her soft skin, his breathing bottomed out. She was perfection.

Her hands found his back, sliding along the slick skin and sleek muscles, and lower. His hands glided along her back to her bottom. Realizing she still wore the pale panties, he peeled them away. His hands went lower. Their kiss deepened as arousal spiked through him and the water perfectly aligned them.

As if they'd done it a million times before, their bodies gracefully merged. The lapping water created a soothing rhythm that grew more and more frantic as need rose until it crested, sending both of them over the edge.

CHAPTER NINE

THEY FLOATED ON the water for a good twenty seconds before either of them could move. Then he caught her elbows again and pulled her to him for another long, lingering kiss.

Marcia let herself fall into it. Passion slowly built between them, but she pushed back, angling herself away from him.

"It's getting chilly."

He laughed. "I didn't notice."

She swam to the edge of the pool and lifted herself out. "I'll race you to my room." She turned and headed for the door.

His confused expression gave way to a hearty laugh. She loved hearing him laugh. Loved seeing him so relaxed and happy. And knew she'd been right the night before. This was why fate brought them together. Not for forever, but for now.

"You have a head start!"

She stopped. Putting her hands on her hips, she frowned. "Okay. To balance things out, I'll grab our clothes. But you have to get the ones still in the pool."

With one quick swoop, she lifted his wet shirt and her dripping dress and raced into the house. She tossed both into the sink as she passed it and ran through the kitchen and hall to the steps. Hearing the door close in the kitchen again, signaling that he was right behind her, she ran up the stairs.

She let the door to her bedroom open and rifled through a box in her bureau for a condom, which she tossed on the bedside table before she pulled down the covers on her bed.

Gloriously naked, he finally made it to her room. Once again wearing his glasses, he spotted the condom and winced. "I guess we got a little carried away out there."

"It's not a big deal." She cleared her throat. "I'm on the pill. And I obviously haven't had sex recently."

He fell to the bed beside her. "Me neither."

"Oh, don't tell me Mr. Affair-No-Relationships hasn't been having some fun."

"It's been a weird few months since we sold the business. The year before that I hadn't had time for a vacation. Not even a weekend trip. My life pretty much revolved around work."

She pulled him down for a kiss. "So I gathered."

She didn't really want to talk and neither did he. It had been so long since she'd been held, caressed...worshipped the way he touched her.

A whirlwind of feelings tried to overtake her, but she flicked them away. For once in her life she didn't want the burden of perfection or the future. Looking for the perfect guy had led her straight into the arms of someone playing a role, pretending to be the real thing so he could gain her trust and then steal from her family.

There would be no more of that in her life.

She didn't know how she'd get herself back into normal relationships, how she'd learn to discern a good guy from a bad guy, but right now, it didn't matter. They liked each other and were good for each other. This was a good thing.

He kissed her neck and she laughed. *A very good thing.*

They played for what seemed like hours, didn't talk, except to say words of happiness, then fell asleep in each other's arms.

Hours later, Trace woke suddenly and sprang up in her bed. *Her bed.*

Morning light came through the window. The sound of her dad's old truck rolled up the vineyard lane.

He jumped out of bed. "Get up! We're late. Your dad's here."

Her eyes opened slowly, sleepily. In the pale morning light, her skin shimmered, her eyes sparkled.

His frenetic search for clothes halted. He bent

down, kissed her thoroughly, then ran to the door. "I'm sorry, but your dress and my shorts are in the kitchen sink. Your dad doesn't always come in but I'm not a lucky person. Today will be the day he pops in for a cup of coffee." Especially if their lateness gave him reason to come searching for them. "I don't want to have to explain a dress and shirt in the sink."

She laughed and he raced to his bedroom for shorts and a T-shirt, which he hopped into on his way downstairs. In the kitchen, he tossed the still-wet clothes into a plastic garbage bag and threw them into the laundry room.

Attempting to make everything appear normal, he hurriedly made a pot of coffee and put two slices of bread in the toaster.

Her dad walked in through the back door. "What's this? We're wearing shorts now?"

"No. I slept in." He nodded toward the coffee maker. "Needed coffee more than I needed a shower. Grab a cup."

"I think I will do that."

His toast popped as her dad retrieved a mug and filled it with coffee, which he left black. Trace eased to the toaster, pulled out his bread and slathered it with butter, then poured himself a cup of coffee.

Antonio smiled at him.

He smiled back. Nerves shimmied through him. Not because he was worried Antonio had seen or guessed something had happened between him and Marcia, but because this was the kind of close call he hadn't thought about the night before. It was archaic and weird to even consider that Antonio would go all medieval on him. But who knew how a dad would react to finding his daughter in bed with—

Holy hell. *He'd awoken in a bed.*

He'd slept through the night!

That was the reason he'd never thought about this scenario. He'd never considered that he'd sleep through the night. He'd assumed he'd wake after twenty minutes.

He scrubbed his hand along the back of his neck.

He'd slept through the night.

"Why you sleep in?"

His gaze jumped to Antonio's. A lie easily slid off his tongue. "One too many glasses of wine, I guess."

Antonio laughed. "One of the hazards of owning thousands of bottles." He peered at Trace. "Though you do look well rested. Not so tired around the eyes." He nudged Trace. "Maybe you need more wine."

Trace only stared at him. It was so unusual for him to sleep through the night he almost couldn't reconcile it in his brain. But he couldn't make too much of it. Especially when he didn't want Marcia's dad thinking too much about the living arrangements here at Giordano Vineyards. And he needed to get dressed because they had work to do.

He finished his toast as Antonio sipped coffee. Then he rose from his seat. "You go ahead out to the wine room and I'll get dressed."

"Don't forget to shower."

Trace peeked at Antonio. "Do I smell that bad?"

He laughed. "No, but you said you didn't shower."

The man had a brain like a steel trap. Another reason to remember to be cautious around him. "Okay." He headed for the door. "Give me twenty minutes."

"You should be done right about when our first tourists arrive."

He pushed on the door. "Great. I'll see you then."

That night, he stayed in the wine room until the tourists were gone. Expecting Marcia to already be in bed, or at least to have eaten, he was surprised to find her in the kitchen.

"No pasta tonight. It's late," she explained. "I was thinking grilled cheese sandwiches."

His stomach growled. He hadn't yet come up with a plan to keep their affair a secret from her dad. But her dad was gone. That worry was something to ponder tomorrow.

"I haven't had a toasted cheese sandwich since I was a kid. I would love one."

"Good. You go get some wine and take it outside. I will bring out sandwiches."

By the time he had a bottle of wine, she was walking out the back door with a plate of sandwiches.

Sitting at the seat he now considered "his" at the outdoor table, he took a sandwich. "Nice night."

She smiled at him. "Yes. Very nice."

He'd be an idiot to misinterpret the gleam in her dark eyes, but his awkward feelings during his encounter with her dad that morning poured through him. Technically, if Antonio discovered their affair, he could think Trace was using Marcia, a woman who'd been hurt so much she was easy prey.

He wasn't sure that he wasn't using her. Though, he had no idea. Everything with her felt different. Special. Original. He'd married so young, then had a spotted relationship with women after that. No real feelings. Just fun. That's what she'd said she wanted and he did too.

All he could do was let this play out.

And hope her dad didn't find out.

They ate their sandwiches talking about their days. When Marcia was done, she rose. She took her wineglass and walked over to a chaise. She sat, stretched out her legs and patted the spot beside her.

"Let's enjoy the night."

As if hypnotized, he rose and slid down on the chaise with her.

"How does our moon compare with yours in Manhattan?"

He snorted. "We rarely see it. Too many tall buildings and light pollution. It has to be big and full before anyone even notices it."

"That's too bad. It's beautiful, don't you think?"

He settled back, got comfortable as he gazed at the moon and the stars twinkling in the dark sky. "Yes. It is beautiful."

She took a breath, nestled beside him. "This is why you bought the place... *Si?*"

"Si." Something about her soft words made him relax again, ease a little farther into the soft cushion.

"We have to be careful not to fall asleep here."

He laughed. "Oh, absolutely. It hit me today that your dad might not be happy with the shift in our relationship."

"Maybe."

"Oh, no *maybe* about it. The last man you guys let into your inner circle robbed you blind and broke your heart."

"You won't break my heart."

He smiled and shook his head. "You're very trusting."

"I trust myself. I'm pretty sure neither one of us believes this is permanent. For now—tonight—" She sat up and looked down at him. "What do you say we just enjoy the stars?"

He studied her beautiful dark eyes. Something

warm and soft shifted through him. The urgency that usually caused him to look for answers, new ways of doing things, new things to do, fluttered away. His limbs relaxed. His head emptied.

He couldn't remember the last time that had happened.

After ten minutes, they began to kiss. Then she rose from the chaise and took his hand, leading him to her room.

Thursday morning, they woke early, ate breakfast and hopped into Trace's car to visit the next two vineyards on Ruth Montgomery's list.

Marcia punched the first address into her phone as he started the car. "This vineyard is two hours away!"

"Is that a problem?"

She thought for a second. "If my parents buy it, they will have to leave their friends."

He laughed. "Is *that* a problem?"

"I don't know. I haven't had time to give it any thought."

His eyes twinkled with mischief. She'd never seen him so happy or so comfortable. Pride filled her. She might not know the depth of his pain, but from the way he'd behaved when he arrived, it had to be deep and strong.

And she helped him forget. If only for a few weeks or a few months. Plus, getting her mind off herself and focusing on someone else was the best thing that had ever happened to *her*. She felt better too. Strong and smart. As capable as she'd felt before Adam.

He caught her hand and brought it to his lips for a light kiss. Her heart all but chugged to a stop at the romance of it. An odd hope filled her chest. She reminded herself that he'd been clear about not wanting a real relationship, and she would honor that.

But she was also aware that things had happened between them naturally. Spontaneously. And he was so different. Enjoying himself as much as she was. Falling into the romance like a man truly smitten.

Questions filled her brain.

What if this was more than two attracted people trying to ease their loneliness, forget their pasts?

What if it was real?

She stopped her thoughts. Not because she didn't want it to be real but because part of her wanted it too much and she knew exactly how hurt she would be if she expected things that couldn't happen. Right now, she was happy. He was happy. And that was what counted.

"Okay, so we'll go look at the vineyard, and if it's great, then we'll think through the problem of your parents having to move so far away. If it's not, then there's no need to think through a problem that doesn't exist."

That was exactly the same way she would handle this relationship. As long as this was working, there was no reason to question it or dissect it.

Relief fluttered through her, an unexpected benefit of no expectations. Details didn't matter. None of it mattered. Only the present moment.

The new vineyards Ruth showed them were a bust. Desperately trying to make a sale, Ruth had them trudge all over the rows of grapes on the last vineyard, clearly hoping something about it would make it a contender. But nothing popped. If anything, the tour made it even more obvious why they wouldn't want it.

By the time they got back to Trace's Maserati, they were tired and hot and had a long trip ahead of them.

He paused three steps away from the car door. "Hey, wanna drive?"

Her eyes widened. "This Maserati? Absolutely."

He tossed her the keys. "Okay."

They switched sides and she slid onto the driver's seat of the sleek sports car. She lovingly caressed the leather steering wheel. "I can't believe you're letting me drive."

"We just had one of the worst days of our lives. Walking in heat. Looking at vineyards that absolutely wouldn't work. I thought this would cheer you up."

Grateful, she smiled at him. He returned her smile. Simply. Easily.

And maybe that was the best thing about no expectations. With no worries of setting precedents, they did what they felt. Not afraid she would expect to always be able to drive, he asked her if she wanted to. Being in the moment, spontaneous, was wonderful.

She cautiously drove down the vineyard lane and onto the country road. Trace pulled out his phone. He loved having given her that gift, but he really wanted her to drive so he could find a place to stay the night. He would ask her opinion on it, but he wasn't armed with enough information to persuade her if she argued. He'd tell her once he found a place. Then he'd have something to tempt her with.

Using his phone, he located a bed-and-breakfast only a few miles up the road.

"Hey, look at this. There's a B&B a mile or so ahead of us."

She paused in enjoying her driving to frown at him. "What?"

"I found a bed-and-breakfast." He sighed. "I'm exhausted. You have to admit that after trudging through that last vineyard you are too. We have a two-hour drive ahead of us. Too long, I think, when there's a place we can rest nearby."

She didn't reply, but her face scrunched.

"Since finding your dad a new vineyard is my mission, I will pay for both rooms."

Her already big eyes widened. "You don't have to pay! I have money!"

Her tone clearly said he'd insulted her, and his brow wrinkled. If she wasn't worried about money, then what was she worried about?

He thought for a second and realized the only thing he'd seen her fear in the weeks he'd known her was the gossip she encountered in town.

But how could she be worried about someone seeing them together when the bed-and-breakfast was a two-hour drive away?

Maybe a friend might tell a friend?

She drove the car into the parking area for the small, quaint bed-and-breakfast, and he opened his mouth to reassure her, then shut it again. How could he assure her no one would find out?

He couldn't.

He almost groaned. He didn't want to drive the hours they needed to get home... But he also didn't want to embarrass her.

Still, wasn't it far-fetched to think a friend of a friend would have a friend who would find out they'd spent the night in a bed-and-breakfast two hours away?

She hopped out of the car and headed for the entrance with him on her heels.

"We'll get separate rooms. Then if anyone finds out, we can tell them about our vineyard search."

"And ruin your plan about having my dad think he decided to buy a vineyard all on his own?"

"Hey, we have a backup story, remember? *I'm* looking for a second vineyard."

She stopped at the door and shook her head. He thought she was going to argue, but she stepped through. As they entered the cool foyer, a man walked through an opening behind a small check-in desk.

"We don't have a reservation. We're hoping you have a vacancy," Trace said.

"*Si. Si.* I will check." He riffled through a book, turning the big pages with a flourish. "Tourists?"

He almost said yes, but despite his easy half-truths with her dad, he wasn't the kind of person to lie. Fortunately, he didn't mind massaging the truth. He could be vague enough that the clerk wouldn't figure out who they were. Especially if they used only one credit card. His. No matter how snippy she got about him paying for their rooms, he would pay.

"We're from a few hours south of here. We went looking at two vineyards, hoping to buy."

The man peeked up. "But no luck?"

"No luck."

"You have luck now though." He turned the book toward Trace. "I have a room for a lovely married couple. Soaking tub. Soft comforter." He smiled.

Trace blinked, then glanced at Marcia, whose only reaction was a widening of her eyes.

The clerk gave her a soft look. "Newlyweds?"

Taking the plunge, not at all unhappy at the clerk's misreading everything, Trace signed the book. "Something like that." He handed his credit card to the older gentleman, who saw his name but not Marcia's.

All problems solved.

They headed upstairs behind the clerk, who finally realized they had no luggage.

Trace said, "We were expecting to go back tonight. Didn't realize how far we'd driven."

"Ah. If you want, I can toss your clothes in the washer."

"No, we'll be fine."

The clerk left, closing the door behind him, and Marcia burst into giggles. "How does it feel to be a newlywed?"

He knew, of course. Her silly question brought back a million feelings. Old emotions about a situation that suddenly seemed so, so far in the past.

"It's not bad," he said, walking over to her, refusing to let his memories mar the moment. He scooped her into his arms and kissed her. "Especially since it comes with you."

"Though we're going to have to put these dirty clothes back on tomorrow morning, I still think it would be a good idea for us to shower first."

"Oh, I do too."

She laughed and led him into a quaint bathroom where he kissed her senseless so neither one of them would think of anything but the current minute.

CHAPTER TEN

THEY WOKE THE next morning to birds chirping outside their window. And wonderfully rested. He'd slept through the night—

Again.

She nestled against his side. Warmth careened through him, but so did contentment. The peace he'd been searching for for years wove through him, calming his nerves, making him feel normal again.

"I'm not ready to go home yet."

He wrapped his arms around her. "Neither am I."

"But we can't stay. We barely have time to get home before Papa and the boys get there."

"I know." But, oh, he wanted to stay. He almost felt he was living a fantasy, something so good, so perfect, it couldn't be real. He glanced at his phone. When he saw the time, his eyes bulged. "Oh, damn. Your dad will be at the vineyard in a little over an hour."

She groaned. "And we have a two-hour drive!"

"Exactly."

He expected her to hop out of bed. Instead, her mood changed, shifted, and she laughed. "Maybe we're thinking about this all wrong." She nuzzled his neck. "He does know how to open and run the wine bar."

His hand slid down her side. "True." He drew in a breath, ridiculously tempted by her softness. "There's only one problem. We would have to explain why we weren't there this morning."

"You do need furniture."

Confused, he looked down into her brown eyes. "What does that have to do with anything?"

"We could say we got up early and went to look at things for the house."

He rolled out of bed before he could be lured into doing something that would only add time to an already iffy schedule. The realization that they would be out-and-out lying to her dad again sent an odd sensation through him.

A knock on the door had him scurrying for his pants. He jumped into them while Marcia raced into the bathroom. When he opened the door, the bed-and-breakfast owner beamed at him over a room service cart.

"I have fruit and coffee."

A bit surprised, Trace said, "Thank you."

The owner winked at him. "On the house, since we suspect you won't be coming down for breakfast."

Trace laughed. "Actually, we won't. We have

to get on the road ASAP. Is there anything I need to sign to check out?"

"No. I have your card number. You can leave whenever." He smiled broadly. "But if I had such a beautiful wife, I wouldn't let this opportunity pass."

Trace chuckled as the older man walked out of the room. He wondered why he was letting such a great opportunity pass. Then he remembered her dad and the lie that just didn't sit right and decided they needed to get moving.

But the owner's comment about Marcia being his wife also hit Trace funny. When he thought *wife*, he thought of Skylar. He couldn't picture Marcia as his wife… But he could picture her as *a* wife.

Somebody's beautiful wife.

A woman a man committed to not because she was gorgeous—though she was. But because she was kind, generous, wonderful.

She came out of the bathroom fully dressed and the sight of her stole his breath. The room immediately filled with light and happiness.

"Aren't you ready?"

He stood like a yutz, barefoot, bare-chested, because his brain had been lollygagging. Stalled because the B&B owner had assumed Marcia was his wife.

He couldn't believe his brain stumbled over that.

But he suddenly realized why it had. If Trace

were in the market for a wife, *she* would be a strong candidate.

He chuckled inwardly at his choice of words and realized why he'd never marry again. No woman would want to be thought of as a strong candidate.

He pulled his shirt over his head and looked under the bed for his socks. "Be ready in two minutes." He peeked up at her again. Her glorious black hair and warm brown eyes. "Pour us a cup of coffee and maybe grab some fruit for the road."

"Okay."

The owner had kindly left both china and paper plates, lovely cups and take-out cups. Marcia poured coffee for them in the take-out cups and gathered some fruit, surreptitiously watching Trace rummage beneath the bed for his socks.

The sadness had been gone from his eyes when she came out of the bathroom. She'd seen peeks of his sorrow the day before, even a glimpse of it that morning, when she was trying to convince him they could stay. But to her great relief, it was gone.

It didn't puzzle her that he had sad days. If she was reading the situation correctly, he'd covered his grief with work, and now that he didn't have the mind-numbing, long hours that running a conglomerate entailed, he had moments when the past sneaked up on him.

She got it. He hadn't fully processed his past.

The loss of a child. The breakdown of a marriage. She didn't know how to help him with that, but she did know how to make him smile. Which, in the end, might be how he would eventually adjust to his losses. Whether he saw it or not, she was good for him. And that was good for her. They were both moving on—

Except just as he had moments of sorrow, she had moments of *what if*. What if this was real? What if they were crazy not to see that?

She shook her head to clear away those thoughts. If it was real, it would last. That was not a question for two people who'd known each other only a few weeks.

The drive back was fun. With the car roof up for safety purposes, they sipped coffee and ate fruit, working not to spill anything on the beautiful leather of his car seats. Though he would groan every time she bobbled a grape and slowed the car's speed when she took a sip of coffee, he also laughed.

She kept the drive light, knowing this was what he needed. Silliness strong enough that he could see life goes on.

He drove the car into the Giordano Vineyards parking lot, easing past buses and rental cars galore.

Trace whistled. "Wow. Looks like our best day ever."

"It's Friday," she reminded him as he pulled into

a parking spot. She opened her door to get out and spoke to him over the roof of his car. "Always a big day."

"I'm going to skip a shower and just jump into my vintner clothes."

He walked around to her side of the car and she smiled at him. The door of the wine room exploded open and Antonio burst out.

"Where the hell were you?"

Trace faced him with a laugh. "Relax, Antonio. We were—"

"You were nowhere in town! The villa was dark and empty all night." He turned his heated gaze on Marcia. "Where were you?" He stalked toward her, his eyes shooting fire. "Wasn't it enough to bring scandal and shame on our family once? Do you plan to live this way?"

Trace stepped in between them. "Okay, let me stop you before you embarrass yourself. We were out looking for—"

She waited expectantly for him to say *furniture*. Instead, after a pause, he said, "Vineyards for you."

Marcia gaped at him. That wasn't the cover story they'd created.

"We'd traveled pretty far the day before and had to stay over."

Looking like a bull ready to charge, her dad faced Trace. "Stay over?"

"A B&B. It was the first thing we came to."

She'd never seen anybody keep his cool in the face of her dad's anger, and her mouth almost fell open in awe.

Trace waited a few seconds for her dad to answer, but Marcia didn't believe he was going to. His eyes were dark spears aimed at her, the poison of accusation smearing the tips. This was it. The big fight she'd always expected to have with her dad. Except it wouldn't be a fight. Anything he had to say would be the truth. She'd fallen victim to a con man. He'd stolen from them. Nearly bankrupted them. And now she was sleeping with Trace.

Anything he said, she deserved.

Trace shook his head. "Earth to Antonio. How did you miss that I just told you we were looking for a vineyard for you?"

Antonio glanced at him, confused. "What?"

Marcia blinked. She didn't know what Trace was doing. But he'd taken her father's attention off her, off the butt kicking she knew she deserved.

Trace pulled his phone out of his pocket and tapped his contacts. "Hey, Ruth. It's Trace Jackson. I think Antonio is finally ready to start looking at vineyards. How about the one with the white gates?"

Marcia held back a gasp. Not only was he taking the heat off her, but he was removing her dad. Not letting him have the screaming fit he so clearly wanted to have.

"That's great." He disconnected the call, caught Antonio's arm and led him to his car.

Marcia stepped out of the way.

"This vineyard needs oodles of work. But—" he pointed to the wine-tasting room entrance "—you've got two healthy young sons in there who could help you fix it up."

Antonio peered back at the wine building. "I do not understand."

"Get in," Trace said amicably. "We won't put the top down so I can explain things to you. But on the way home, top down. You're gonna love this car."

Marcia stared after them as they drove away. She finally noticed that she hadn't been invited along, even though she had been a big part of building Giordano Vineyards—

But maybe she didn't need to be a part of building the new vineyard? Maybe what *she* needed was to separate herself. Her entire life she'd been in training to take over the family vineyard, but it came at a price. She'd been so focused, so sheltered, that she'd fallen victim to a charlatan. And now that she was finally finding herself, finding her footing, she didn't want to go backward.

She didn't want to lose her family, but she did want to be herself. Her real self.

Whether he knew it or not, Trace had just saved her. And not with a lie or made-up story. Simply by forcing her dad to move forward.

Forcing her to move forward too.

By separating her from the new vineyard.

Trace Jackson, Mr. Fix-It, had to be the most amazing man she'd ever met.

She squeezed her eyes shut as the questions from the bed-and-breakfast poured through her again. *Was this real?*

She groaned. It almost didn't matter if it was real. She was falling in love. How could she not? The man was wonderful.

But that was wrong. So wrong.

If she didn't collect herself, she was going to end up hurt when their time together ended—

Unless it didn't end?

Unless he did all these nice things for her because he was falling in love too?

CHAPTER ELEVEN

TRACE WAITED ONLY until they were out of the lane to Giordano Vineyards before he pulled the car to the side of the road and faced Antonio.

"You will never yell at Marcia like that again."

Antonio's eyes narrowed and his chin lifted. "She is my daughter."

"And your employee. Technically when she got involved with the guy who stole from you, she was more employee than daughter."

Antonio snorted.

Trace paused a second. Nothing Marcia had told him had ever been in confidence. Still, he thought of her feelings, what needed to be said, what didn't, before he spoke.

"Do you know she was trying to buy the Giordano Vineyards back from me?"

Antonio peered over at him. "She doesn't have that kind of money."

"She says she has a friend who could lend it to her."

Antonio inhaled sharply. "Janine." He shook

his head. "But her mother is sick… If I remember correctly, she has cancer." He scrubbed his hand across his mouth. "Marcia wouldn't bother them in their time of trouble."

"That's probably the only reason she hasn't actually made an offer."

Antonio gave him a confused look. "And you would have sold it back to her?"

"Nope. Sorry. A deal is a deal. But it only took me a few days to realize you weren't mad at Marcia for the embezzling mess as much as you are angry with yourself."

When Antonio said nothing, Trace said, "You trusted him too."

"*Si.*"

"So, stop being angry with her. Or projecting your anger with yourself onto her and do something."

Antonio laughed and speared him with a sly look. "You mean like buy another vineyard."

"You're still young. You've got two healthy sons. And you are not happy as a retired man."

He snorted.

"Are you?" Trace prodded. "You come to work for me every day as if you can't decide what to do with yourself."

Antonio straightened. "I'm helping you get established."

"Pfft." Trace shook his head. "I could hire thirty people to run Giordano Vineyards."

"You would lose money."

"And I wouldn't care. Because I have more than enough for three lifetimes." He peered at Antonio. "Look. I love having you and your sons around, but I don't need you and you *do* need something else in your life."

He turned and restarted the car's engine, heading for the vineyard with the white gates, which was only a few miles away. "I'd originally nixed the vineyard we're going to see, but I think I spoke too soon."

"Why did you not think it right?"

"It's run-down. Really run-down. But the more vineyards I saw, the more I realized nothing else had quite the right set of specifications."

"*You* know what *I* need."

Trace laughed. "I'm a fixer," he said, and for once he didn't hate the sound of it on his tongue. "I see things objectively."

Antonio sniffed. "You see my daughter objectively?"

"Of course. I could tell on day one that she was determined to make it up to you that she'd lost your vineyard." He peeked at Antonio as he sped down the road. "She's got a lotta spunk, that one. Told me she'd run me off in less than a year."

Antonio laughed.

"That's why I involved her in the search for a new vineyard for you. She needed to feel that she was doing something to make up for hurting you."

Antonio said nothing.

"She's a good person."

"Which is why I don't want you to hurt her."

The comment surprised Trace, but when he considered it, he didn't know why he thought it had come out of the blue. He wasn't the only perceptive human being in the world. Though he and Marcia had been careful, discreet, fathers had an instinct.

"I'm not going to hurt her."

But he was. He *knew* he was. That was what all the memories of Skylar were about. Except in this case, he wasn't the one who got hurt. He was the passive, not committed one, in it only for the fun side of the affair.

Things he hadn't wanted to admit to himself shuffled through his brain. How Skylar loved rebelling. How she'd loved his devotion to her. How she'd been able to leave their marriage without pain, without a sense of a loss of anything except their son. When Joshua had died, the fun had gone out of her rebellion and been replaced by the stark and terrible reality that real life wasn't always a joyride.

Hating how those thoughts pinched his chest and made him want to punch something, he shut them down. Shoved them aside. Refused to give them space in his brain.

"Yes. You are going to hurt her," Antonio assured

him. "Maybe not this week or this month or even this year. But you will move on."

"I don't want to move on. I like it here. I like the peace and quiet."

"And the slow pace?" Antonio laughed. "You tell me I need something more, but what about you? How long until you want to get your hands on another billion-dollar opportunity? How long until a man with your education and instincts starts looking at every business he sees as a chance to make another big score?"

Trace squirmed in his seat. "So far I haven't wanted one."

Antonio snorted. "So far... That's precious. You might as well admit that something is going to tempt you away eventually. And knowing that, any relationship you have with my daughter is temporary."

Trace bit his lower lip to keep from lying. He'd put this man on the ropes professionally, was taking him by the hand, telling him he needed to buy another vineyard, grab the reins of his life. He could not tell him he wasn't going to hurt his daughter any more than he could profess that he wouldn't leave Tuscany one day, wouldn't find an opportunity that would lure him back to luscious Manhattan, where he could get a pizza at any time of the day or night, go to the theater or the Metropolitan Museum of Art.

Except...

He slept when he was with Marcia.

But he also slept when he was working his brain to exhaustion. And there might come a time when a company, a challenge, a chance to be himself again might tempt him more than Marcia.

Oh, God. He *was* using her.

Trace and Antonio returned to Giordano Vineyards a little after five. Antonio had loved White Gates Vineyards—he'd decided to name it that because it fit—and he'd instructed Ruth to make an offer. The real estate agent for the vineyard owner was excited that someone was finally interested, and claimed the owner was eager to sell. So, they'd waited in Ruth's office until the acceptance came through.

The happy pair walked into the wine-tasting room together, all smiles. No hint that Trace all but vibrated with confusion and self-loathing about his relationship with Marcia.

"Hey, everybody," Antonio shouted, commanding the attention of the thirty or so people in the room, including his sons. "I just bought another vineyard."

His sons' eyes popped, but the tourists in the crowd began slapping his back, congratulating him and toasting the new venture.

Trace laughed. Despite their conversation about Marcia as they drove to White Gates, their afternoon had been fun. He liked Antonio. He enjoyed his happiness.

Another bus pulled in and the excitement of the moment took a back seat to work. Trace welcomed the new group while Matteo and Roberto wrote orders from the group getting ready to leave. He and Antonio worked side by side, laughing, involving tourists in their fun, as they poured samples of each kind of wine.

It was eight o'clock before he was able to get away. Antonio promised he and his sons would close the room after the last group left. He hated leaving Antonio with work that was essentially his and his alone now. But all day, he'd gotten shots of memory that about killed him.

Every time he thought about Antonio's accusation that he'd leave, which made him realize he was using Marcia, his brain would jump to Skylar, the new way he was beginning to see her. He couldn't hate her. He'd never hated her, not even for leaving him. She'd been eighteen at the time. *Eighteen.* Too young to bear the burdens of a lost child when their relationship had been nothing but a rebellion against her parents.

He'd loved *her.* Purely. Innocently. He was the one who'd made the big plan to get married when she'd discovered she was pregnant. With time providing perspective, he could remember how her agreement had been a wobbly one. He couldn't hate her for something the Mr. Fix-It in him had orchestrated.

Particularly since his manipulations hadn't gotten the good outcome his older, wiser self got when he intervened to fix business problems. The end of his marriage had been an unmitigated disaster.

Skylar's allegiance clearly hadn't lain with him. A few days after Joshua's death, when he'd realized she wasn't coming back to their apartment, he'd called her and forced her to talk with him. She'd calmly, rationally explained that without their child there was no reason for them to be together. He'd argued that that was her parents talking, but something had changed in her voice. He'd heard a tiredness…

In a way, he supposed he'd always known she didn't love him.

So why did it still torment him?

Twelve years had gone by. He'd spent the bulk of them fine. Busily building his real life.

Why was all this tormenting him now? He could say that without the work of the corporation his brain had too much time to think. But there was more. He knew there was more. And if he used Marcia to stop the pain, would he actually delay figuring all this out?

Not hearing a sound in the house when he entered, he took the steps two at a time and ambled down the hall to the master suite, where he showered and changed into comfortable clothes.

When he returned downstairs, the place was silent, confusing him. He made himself a sandwich in the kitchen, which he took to the patio. He saw Marcia lying on a chaise by the pool and knew why the house had been silent.

She'd been out here.

Her tiny bikini hid nothing. Moonlight sparkling off the water in the pool brought back memories of the first time they'd made love. How he'd picked her up and jumped into the warm water with her.

His breaths bubbling in his chest, he sat on the chaise beside hers. Memories of Skylar colliding with memories of Marcia vibrated through him. He'd never before compared another woman to Skylar.

And he wondered if that wasn't also a piece of this puzzle.

"Hey."

Her eyes opened and she smiled at him. Her face was perfection. Dark, sensual eyes. A pert nose. Full, lush lips.

"Hey."

He swallowed a swell of emotion that threatened to overwhelm him. Touching her velvet skin took him to another place. Sleeping next to her brought him peace.

But wasn't that actually the problem?

She gave him the one thing he'd longed for—rest—when maybe what his brain really needed was to be pushed to the limit, forced to face a dark demon that robbed him of sleep but wouldn't show itself.

Not able to think that through now, he pushed the horrifying thought away. What more could he possibly have to face than the loss of a child?

"Your dad bought White Gates Vineyards."

She sat up. "The first one we looked at?"

"Yep. He named it White Gates Vineyards."

"Oh, my gosh! He really did it?"

Trace caught her gaze. "And he's happy."

Her eyes softened. "He is?"

"He is. I explained my reasoning for looking for a new vineyard for him and he agreed. I told him that the way he spent so much time at Giordano Vineyards proved he needed something to do. I also told him that creating a second successful vineyard would get him beyond the mistake of trusting Adam."

"How'd he take it?"

"He listened." And threw accusations back at Trace about his daughter. But Trace wouldn't tell her that. A conversation a man has with the father of the woman he's sleeping with was a delicate thing. A father always knew his daughter would make her own choices, but the man sleeping with that daughter always knew the dad would kick his ass—or somehow make his life miserable—if he hurt her. Dads didn't like daughters setting themselves up to be hurt by a con man...or a rogue. He might not be a con man, but he supposed he fell into the rogue category.

Skylar's dad had chosen to freeze him out. And in the end, it had worked. When push came to shove, Skylar went home.

Marcia's dad had simply called him out. And that was working too. He couldn't go on sleeping with her now that he knew he'd eventually hurt her. As Antonio said, he'd leave someday. He'd be the Skylar in their relationship.

Not because he was cold and heartless, or too young to make a choice, but because until he really understood what his brain was trying to tell him, he knew he didn't deserve someone like Marcia. Sweet, fierce and longing to make a future, she would want children. She didn't have to say it. Her love and loyalty to family said it for her.

While he couldn't even think about children without cold dread washing over him, freezing his brain on one thought: he'd failed as a father.

He could not tie her to him.

He finished his sandwich and rose from the chaise. "Anyway, just thought you'd want to know."

Marcia's head tilted. "Where are you going?"

His heart stuttered. Every fiber of his being wanted to stay. He loved being with her. Loved how he felt with her. But if a man who could not commit continued sleeping with a woman who needed a commitment, he would be leading her

on. And he was not the kind of guy who led someone on or lived a lie.

"Inside. Maybe I'll get a beer. I don't know."

His words seemed to hang in the air, creating
an odd sensation that fluttered through him. He
was saying one thing, when he wanted another.
He was so accustomed to taking her in his arms,
laughing with her, making love like goofy pup-
pies, that it seemed wrong to leave.

But he couldn't stay. Not because Antonio had
been correct. That he would someday find another
project, hire sufficient staff for Giordano Vineyards and leave without a backward glance. Because of Marcia. He did not want to be the source
of new pain for her—

"Stay with me."

Temptation rose again. But that was the problem. She was perfect. Easy for a man to desire.

And he was nothing. The guy who sweet-talked
his girlfriend into marrying him. How could he
ever believe he deserved to be trusted? How could
he ever trust *himself* to be even a halfway decent
partner to a woman who merited so much more?

He silenced his longings, the voice that begged
him to take a chance. On what? On forever? He
would never have forever. He'd had that shot and
he'd blown it.

Was that what his brain wanted him to remember? That he'd lost his chance? That his life was
best spent working?

Which would make Antonio right. His psyche was telling him he needed to find new work, a bigger company to run. Not to mess around with a woman who merited better.

"We have a busy day tomorrow. At some point, I think you and your dad need to talk. Then your dad and I need to make preliminary plans for what to do with White Gates. I'll need some sleep."

He shrugged and almost turned to go into the house. But he saw the hurt in her dark eyes and bent down to kiss her. "I'll see you in the morning."

"Okay."

He walked inside the villa reminding himself that he'd finally gotten this family back on its feet. He would not do anything to jeopardize that. He wouldn't use Marcia. He would end their relationship before she was so involved that she got hurt when he found another business deal, grew tired of Tuscany or simply decided to return to Manhattan.

Because it no longer seemed far-fetched that he should leave. In fact, going back to Manhattan might be the answer he'd been searching for all along.

CHAPTER TWELVE

MARCIA WOKE THE next morning disoriented. Without opening her eyes, she reached for Trace, but he wasn't there. The day before had been exhausting. Her dad had all but accused them of having an affair—which they were, but it wasn't something anyone liked shouted across a crowded vineyard parking lot packed with tourists.

Trace had needed to get his bearings. She totally understood.

She left her bed, showered and dressed in a soft floral shirtwaist dress. She also had some things to adjust to. Her dad was back to being a businessman, and her brothers would be leaving. She and Trace had tons of work to do. It was time to get her head in the game.

He wasn't in the kitchen when she arrived, but a pot of coffee told her he'd been there. She grabbed a mug and filled it, then walked to her workspace. As she suspected, Trace and her dad were in her dad's old office. Trace sat at the desk, his fingers on the keyboard of a laptop. Her dad stood over his shoulder, pointing at something on the screen.

When she closed the door, Trace looked up. "We're creating a budget. Wanna join us?"

She took a soft breath, her gaze jumping to her father. "I don't know—"

"Please," her dad said. "We could use your help."

Her heart skipped a beat. She knew this was as close to an apology as she'd ever get. But acceptance, a welcome back to the fold, was better than a platitude.

She walked to the desk, glanced at the screen and began giving recommendations. Adam might have gotten their first loan and created the renovation plans, but she'd worked with him on hiring a general contractor and organizing a huge revitalization of Giordano Vineyards. She'd also had to assume his end of the responsibilities, including getting a second loan, when he skipped town. Her former fiancé might have hurt them, but she'd gained experience, and now she, her dad and Trace would put it to good use.

Her shame and apprehension fell away and were replaced by a burst of self-esteem. She didn't need Trace pointing the way anymore. She could do this. Herself.

She also didn't *need* Trace personally. So much stronger than when she'd met Adam, she knew the difference between hero worship and real feelings, and what she felt for Trace was deeper, richer, more profound than anything she'd ever felt for Adam.

Her heart caught. She tried to tell herself she'd come to yesterday's conclusion that she loved him too quickly...

But that was a lie. These feelings were strong and real.

She loved him.

Was it another mistake? He never said he loved her. He'd all but closed the door on a future. She'd started their affair knowing it would be temporary. She'd even told him that. How had she fallen in love?

She fought the urge to squeeze her eyes shut. She couldn't think about this now. There was work to be done. She needed her focus, first, to help her dad create a plan of action for the new vineyard. Second, to work with Trace to hire the people they would need to keep Giordano Vineyards bustling and prosperous once her father and brothers moved on.

Her dad pondered every choice with the enthusiasm of a man who'd gotten a second chance at life, but Trace was all business. No smiles. No chitchat. No joking around.

At first, she chalked that up to the presence of her father and Trace's sincere desire to help him become successful.

But when she left for lunch, he didn't follow.

He went into the wine-tasting room. He helped her brothers work with tourists until late, a common occurrence on weekends.

Her thoughts tripped over into the situation that had tried to overwhelm her that morning. They had begun their affair with no promises. She wasn't allowed to change her mind. Particularly since he was behaving differently. Now that they had handled her father's troubles, he'd pulled away. As if her family's problems had been the draw, not her.

The conclusion emptied her heart, hollowed out her chest.

She couldn't be angry with him. She'd been the one to set the terms. He'd given her a couple of weeks of fun, of happiness.

But she could be angry with herself for letting it become more than he'd intended.

More than *they'd* intended.

Deciding not to dwell on it, but to wait to see how things went after her dad and brothers left, she showered, changed into a simple nightshirt and grabbed the novel she'd been reading from the bedside table.

Minutes of waiting became an hour.

One hour turned into two.

She fell asleep reading and woke alone again.

This time, there was no waffling, no confusion about what was going on. He was absolutely avoiding the personal side of the relationship.

She thought of Adam, how she'd been so blind, and for a split second was proud she wasn't such a chump this time. But the loss hit her before she could stop it. The thought that she would work with him every day and never touch him, never kiss him, never have another intimate talk.

She reminded herself they had made no promises. They'd mutually decided to live in the moment, and now he was walking away.

She either had to accept that or be a chump again.

And that was one lesson she'd vowed never to repeat.

She would not be a chump. She would not be the weeping woman, cast aside by a man. She'd entered their affair with her head high. She would keep it high.

Monday morning, Trace worked with Antonio. The all-cash offer for White Gates might get Antonio the vineyard, but he'd need a loan to make repairs to buildings and grapevines that had been abandoned.

After creating the long list of repairs and a spreadsheet with the estimated cost to make them, Trace sat back in his desk chair. "I'm lending you the cash."

Antonio waved his hand in dismissal. "You've done enough."

"No bank is going to give you a no-interest loan."

"So why would *you*?"

"Because we're friends."

Antonio pondered that for a few seconds. "Say more."

"Hey, we're two guys who own vineyards a few miles apart. An alliance works for us."

Antonio chuckled. "True."

"So, let me call my lawyers and get papers ready."

Antonio grinned. "I would argue, but you would argue more. So, I concede. I will take your loan. But it *is* a loan. Not a gift."

Trace held out his hand and they shook on it. "Okay. I'll also have the lawyer create a payment schedule."

Antonio left for lunch, but Trace didn't follow. When he didn't sleep, he didn't seem to get hungry. He headed into the wine-tasting room to do his fair share.

In the early evening, Roberto and Matteo took pity on him and Antonio and shooed their dad home even as they told Trace he looked too tired to be nice to tourists. He laughed, but he also didn't leave.

After ten, he ambled into the house, made a sandwich and took it to the master suite, eating it as he shucked his clothes.

The food made him feel marginally better. But

he didn't wait to see if he could sleep. He headed for the pool patio. The dimmed lights provided enough illumination that he made his way to the first table. He sat, but a movement to the right caught his attention.

He glanced up and saw Marcia sleeping on the chaise.

Tonight, she wasn't wearing a bikini. A big T-shirt fell to her knees. He laughed. Only on Shortie-McShort Marcia would a T-shirt cover her from neck to knees.

He walked over. "Hey, sleepyhead. Unless you're planning on staying here all night, you should go upstairs."

She took a long breath and stretched. Trace's heart stumbled. She looked so sweet, so inno-cent…and yet somehow so sexy. Lifting her arms above her head, she stretched the T-shirt enough that it molded itself to her breasts, her tiny waist, her round hips.

He blew his breath out in a long sigh, forc-ing his thoughts back where they belonged. He was bowing out before he hurt her. He'd made too many mistakes when it came to romance and didn't deserve the kind of love she would give him. Total. Complete. And oh, so sweet.

He shook her shoulder. "I mean it. It gets cold out here at night."

"Just a few more minutes, Mama."

He laughed. "I'm not your mom."

"You sure sound like it."

He laughed and, realizing she was more awake than he'd thought, he put out his hand. "Come on. Let me help you up."

She took a breath, opened her eyes. For twenty seconds she held his gaze.

Everything inside Trace stilled. He wanted to sit beside her on the chaise, toss the T-shirt and make love in the moonlight.

She did too. He could see it in her eyes, sense it in her hesitancy.

He took a breath.

She took a breath.

He wasn't entirely sure what he'd do if she made the first move. Part of him wished she would. Wished she'd say or do something—anything— that he could blame for his inability to resist her.

But she said nothing. She didn't even take the hand he'd extended. She shifted on the chaise so she could rise without his help.

Then she headed for the back door. "Good night, Trace."

He swallowed. "Good night."

The door opened and she walked inside the house.

Longing ruffled through him. But, tonight, she'd been the one to walk away. He loved her strength. Loved that she probably realized he'd ended their affair, but she wasn't pouting or arguing. She'd simply moved on.

He frowned. He didn't know any of that. He hadn't told her about the chat with her dad. For all he knew, *she'd* ended the affair.

The thought burned through him like a hot knife through butter.

He told himself that was crazy. The end had been sensible. It didn't matter who stopped things. Everything that was happening was good. Right.

He took a long breath, then another to quell the pain. He told himself they hadn't been together long enough for him to feel this kind of loss.

Ignoring all of it, he walked back to the patio table, but his thoughts wouldn't leave him. He could picture Marcia and a couple of cute kids playing in the pool.

He frowned, staring at the moonlight twinkling off the pool. If he went back to Manhattan, she'd remain general manager of Giordano Vineyards and, of course, he'd insist she live in the villa. She and her kids would swim in the pool. Laughing. Happy.

His heart froze. His breathing stopped. But he dispatched the pictures to the far corner of his brain. He didn't need to envision what he'd be missing. Part of him already knew.

The next morning, she was in the kitchen when he stumbled in after forty-five minutes of sleep.

She looked sleek and professional with her hair gathered on top of her head and a slim yellow dress riding her curves. She smiled, said, "Good morning," then carried a mug of coffee out the back door, probably on her way to her office.

When the door closed behind her, he whistled. "Holy hell. That woman is on fire."

And he was resisting her. Not because he was strong, but for her. He hadn't needed to go so far as to picture her with another man's children, but he got the gist of it. He wasn't the only one moving on.

The thought stung, but it was yet another thing he had to get accustomed to. And he could not do something foolish before his time at Giordano Vineyards was up. They'd spent the past weeks ensuring Antonio's future and neglected his own business. He had a few more days' work for White Gates before he could shift back to Giordano Vineyards. So he had to suck it up.

Still, the sense of loss vibrated through him, along with fear that he'd have to watch her fall in love with someone else. Ignoring both, he headed to his office, thanking God there were one-year and five-year plans to create for White Gates Vineyards that morning. Antonio was taking his wife to tour the vineyard, so Trace would have something to occupy his mind other than Marcia moving on without him.

His plan to get his focus off what he was missing seemed like it would work, until he remembered Marcia sat in the office in front of his. That was good for when he had questions, but bad when their hands brushed, or when he couldn't keep his eyes off her. She met with suppliers and he surreptitiously watched her sweet-talk them into giving her a better deal. He watched as she had a video call with a graphic artist, wanting to surprise her parents with the perfect logo for White Gates Vineyards.

When the artist disappeared from her computer screen, he rose from his seat and leaned against the door frame between the two rooms. "You're very kind."

She sniffed a laugh. "You wouldn't help your parents if they bought a new business?"

He frowned. "My dad doesn't have that kind of ambition."

"Maybe this is why you hijacked my dad."

He laughed. "I didn't hijack him." He shrugged. "He's my friend."

"I'm not concerned about your love for spending time with my dad as much as I'm curious about your distance from your parents."

He walked from the doorway to sit on the corner of her desk. There was no reason for secrets between them. He intended to go back home, and she'd be moving on without him. In some ways, he actually believed he owed her more explanation about his life, so she'd see his leaving was for the best.

"The last time I was home, my dad said something that about flattened me."

"Must have been something awful."

He picked up her pen, then caught her gaze. "He said my son's death was a blessing in disguise."

Her breathing jerked, so when she spoke, the word came out in a horrified gasp. "What?"

He pretended indifference. "I know. It was hard to hear." He looked down, then caught her gaze again. "My mother tried to explain that what my dad meant was that my ex and I had both moved on and become very successful."

"I'm sure that's true."

"It might have been what he meant, but it's not what he said, and what he said took me so much by surprise I reacted viscerally, from the gut."

"Of course you did! You loved your son. You *miss* your son."

"I do miss my son, but not in the way you might think." He sighed and looked her in the eye again. "I'm not nuts. I don't think about him all the time, but sometimes I miss who he could have been. I miss the chance to teach him how to throw a ball. I miss that wonderful moment when you realize your kid is gifted in math or good with pets or kind to other kids. I long to see who he might have been."

"That makes sense."

"Really?" He snorted. "*Twelve years* have gone by. This sudden burst of yearning makes *no* sense."

"You said yourself that it started when you

had time on your hands to think about it. Maybe avoiding it for twelve years only delayed it."

He shifted on her desk. That's what he'd thought. But now instinct was telling him it was something more, even as it told him he could talk about it with Marcia. She'd always been candid with him. Honest. Open. Never judging.

And maybe that's why she tempted him so much.

"I did say that."

"So why don't you believe it?"

He tapped her pen on the desk. "I have a sense that it's something more."

"More?"

He shrugged, not wanting to talk about this anymore because he suddenly felt foolish. "You know... I'm probably looking for something that isn't there. Just as you said, I was fine until I stopped working."

She laughed. "You are a very smart guy. A perceptive guy. You should take your own advice. Listen to your own reason."

He pulled in a slow breath. Regardless of what he'd said to Marcia, his reason insisted there was more behind his inability to sleep than lack of things to do. He had tons of work to do with White Gates and Giordano Vineyards...yet he hadn't slept the night before—

"We should do something fun tonight. Maybe go to Florence for dinner."

Her shift of topic surprised him so much he blinked. "I don't want to entertain myself to make things go away."

"Oh, really, Antonio?"

He frowned at her.

"My father did not want to buy another vineyard to make himself feel better over losing this one. You forced him." She rose from her seat. "So tonight I'm forcing you to do the thing you really need. Relax. Be ready to drive me to Florence tonight at six. Dress up. We're going somewhere nice."

With that, she picked up her coffee mug and walked out of her office.

He watched her go. Half amused, half confused. It was interesting that she didn't try to talk him out of his grief or even tell him it was time to move on. She'd seen him floundering and made plans for dinner. Technically, she'd thrown what he'd done with her dad back at him. She'd made the plan and guided him to it.

He laughed and returned to Antonio's office—now his office, he supposed—to finish his work.

Her dad arrived at three and Trace showed him the plans for White Gates. He approved, liking how Trace had gone back into Giordano Vineyards' history and mimicked a lot of what Antonio had done the first time around.

"Except, I didn't have so much cash." He shook

his head, remembering. "I was always going to the bank for money."

Trace glanced at the old records that he had spread out on the desk. "Every five years isn't always."

"No. But I was never debt free. I'd pay off a loan and get another."

"To build things up." He glanced at his watch, saw it was almost five and rose. Clasping Antonio's shoulder for a quick squeeze, he said, "We'll refine those plans tomorrow after you have a chance to think them through."

Antonio said, "Thank you."

"For helping a friend?" He batted his hand. "No thanks necessary."

"Thanks are always necessary. Appreciation and respect make the world go round."

He hadn't thought of it like that, but he supposed Antonio was right.

So why was he going out with this man's daughter again? Thoughts of their evening together had about ruined his concentration that afternoon. Especially when he saw Marcia leaving early, obviously to get ready. His nerves had spiked. His thoughts had spiraled. He'd had trouble keeping his mind on his discussions with Antonio.

But he couldn't talk himself into refusing her invitation.

Not because they'd been lovers, but because he

liked her. They were *friends* too. He wasn't merely friends with Antonio. He and Marcia were friends.

Walking into the villa, he reminded himself of his plan to keep his distance but decided that a nice night out, not as lovers, but as friends, might be exactly what they needed to complete the transition.

Marcia tried not to be nervous as she descended the steps to the foyer, where Trace awaited her. He wore a dark suit, white shirt and aqua tie. With his dark hair slicked back and his hands tucked into his pants pockets, he looked casually sexy.

Her heart stuttered but she told herself to stop being silly. Mr. Fix-It had done everything he'd intended. He'd found her dad a new vineyard. He'd helped her get back to being confident and strong. Now someone needed to help him.

She'd seen the confusion that overtook him that afternoon when he spoke of his son. She'd seen his difficulty keeping his focus. Tonight, she would provide him with a pleasant-distraction evening. No romance. No pressure. Just a nice time.

At the bottom of the steps, he caught her hand and brought it to his lips, kissing the knuckles. "Am I going to have to fight off men who will try to steal you?"

Her heart knocked against her ribs. The thought that he might be jealous filled her with hope that she'd misread the past few days. But deep down she knew she hadn't.

So, she went along with his teasing. "What a delicious idea."

He opened the villa door for her. "Delicious?"

"Oh, come on. It would be a hoot to have men fighting over me. Let me have some fun."

He laughed. "Now, isn't that a welcome change in attitude?"

Her heart drooped. She loved his teasing, but the way he had no problem with her being with other men was oh, so hard to take. Still, she wasn't a child. He was done with their affair. She might not know why, but she knew he'd withdrawn. And she also knew he was going through something difficult.

If it killed her, she would give him a lovely, happy evening to ease a bit of his sorrow and his confusion over that sorrow.

They drove to the city, top down, air blowing around them. She led him along the crowded Florence sidewalk to the restaurant. The street smelled of the earth and delicious food, especially freshly baked bread. The sun had gone down, but the heat of the day remained, giving the air a feel that was unique to Tuscany. Her cares melted away. Happiness bubbled inside her.

She'd forgotten how much she loved Florence. After confirming their reservations with the hostess, they were escorted to a table outside. The lights of the city blinked at them.

"I'm sorry," she said, as they were seated. "Beyond all those twinkling lights are mountains. It's too late for the breathtaking view."

"No worries." He toyed with his wineglass. "The view from where I'm sitting is gorgeous."

Her heart squeezed with longing that she had to squelch. Flirting Trace was back. But this dinner, this trip away from the vineyard, wasn't about her. It was about him. He liked to flirt. If it was part of how he forgot his troubles, she would let him.

The waiter arrived with a bottle of wine. She knew it was expensive from the label, but Trace didn't even blink. The waiter poured two glasses and left menus.

Trying to be subtle, she said, "I'm paying for this dinner."

He laughed. "Seriously?"

"Yes!" She thought for a second, then said, "In your normal life, you pay for everything, don't you?"

He shrugged. "I have the money. Lots of people I know don't."

She sat up in her seat. "Well, you're not paying tonight. I asked you out. I pay." Realizing what she'd said, she squeaked. "Not that I'm saying this is a date." She felt her face redden. "It's not."

He reached across the table and took her hand. "Relax."

She sucked in a breath. He was right. Antsy, nervous, guilt-ridden Marcia was gone. This was not the time to revive her. "Yes. Let's both relax."

They talked like friends as the waiter brought several courses of dinner. The moon rose. The night sounds changed. Even the dining area of the restaurant had a hushed reverence to it, as the city slowed down, getting ready to sleep.

As they drove home, they talked some more about her parents, her life. Her teen years seemed to particularly amuse him, and she almost asked about his…about stupid teenage things he'd done… Then she remembered he'd gotten his girl-friend pregnant at eighteen, married her and ulti-mately lost his child. Careful not to go there, she asked about how he'd met the friends he'd gone into business with.

"Harvard. I seriously studied. They goofed off. But when the time came, and the opportunity was right, Wyatt borrowed a hundred million dollars from his parents to buy the two grocery store chains that started us off."

She gaped at him. "He borrowed a hundred million dollars?"

"For two grocery store *chains*. Each chain had over thirty stores. That kind of business doesn't come cheap." He gave her the side-eye. "Plus, he borrowed it from his parents. Which turned out to be great incentive. He absolutely could not fail."

"I suppose not. A hundred million dollars is a lot of money."

"It wasn't about the money. This was about his dad's wealthy family calling him a slacker."

"Interesting."

"He had something to prove."

"So, he put together a good team to make sure he succeeded."

"Exactly."

She smiled at him. She loved how he loved his friends. Respected them. "Have they set a time to visit?"

"No." He paused. "I haven't gotten furniture yet."

She laughed with glee. "Have they ever heard of a hotel? They don't have to stay with you to visit you."

He frowned. "I guess not."

"Let's arrange it."

"Okay."

Content, Trace glanced over at her and his empty heart filled. He loved when someone saw something he didn't. But he also liked that she really had paid. That she didn't make him feel bad that their affair had ended. It felt like balance. Like the whole world didn't rest on his shoulders.

The urge to reach over and take her hand whispered through him. He ignored it. But the light from the dash illuminated her face, her red dress,

her shapely legs, and his breath shivered into his lungs. He'd touched every inch of her, but now, suddenly, he wasn't allowed.

That part seemed off. Like a piece of a puzzle that fits in the available space but doesn't match the colors around it.

She talked nonstop for the rest of the ride home. Mostly drawing out information about Cade and Wyatt, then deciding on the best places to take them when they visited.

She made them sound like a team and Trace licked his suddenly dry lips. Aside from a business partnership, he'd never been a part of a team. He and Skylar certainly weren't a team. He'd always felt a bit of distance with his parents and his sisters. But Marcia's lovely, lilting voice flowed through him like cool water to quench the thirst of a man who lived in a desert. He didn't feel alone. Or lonely. A quiet contentment filled his soul.

He almost hated it when the Giordano Vineyards sign came into view. He slowed his speed as they drove down the long lane, delaying the inevitable end of their trip. But they were in the parking lot soon enough. The car stopped. Their evening was over.

They got out, her face beaming with happiness, and he wondered if his face looked that joyful, that content.

To keep his hand from reaching for hers, he busied himself loosening his tie as they walked to the front door. He took off his jacket and rolled his shirtsleeves as they ambled down the hall to her bedroom.

When they reached it, he stopped with her. "Thank you. I know you wanted to help me keep my mind off the past, and it worked."

"You are not the only Mr. Fix-It."

"Actually, I think you'd be Ms. Fix-It."

She laughed. His quiet soul warmed again. Because they'd been intimate, his body was having difficulty understanding why he couldn't kiss her. Why he couldn't touch her, lie down with her, sleep with her—

Because he had troubles. Something about his past had a hold on him and wouldn't let go. If he couldn't escape it in such a beautiful place as Tuscany, he was beginning to worry it would always haunt him. He was lost, confused and wounded enough that he'd never be able to give her what she needed. A solid marriage. Kids.

Joshua popped into his mind…then his failures.

She placed her palm on his cheek. "Stop thinking. Don't drag yourself back to the past."

He swallowed hard. "Easy for you to say."

"No. Easy for you to say too."

His eyes searched hers. "I could say anything I wanted, but that wouldn't make it real. What's real is what sits inside my chest every time I think of my son…my failures."

"Maybe tonight, don't think of them."

He swallowed hard. He'd give anything for his thoughts to stop cascading back to his past.

"I think you walked away from us because your past makes you believe you will hurt me." Her head tilted. "But what if I hurt you?"

He laughed.

She shook her head. "So much pride."

"It's not pride."

"Silly man. You are not perfect. I am not perfect. Life is not perfect. One of these days I could walk away from you. You don't know that I won't. Neither one of us can tell the future, yet you live it in your head, thinking through every possible bad thing and running from them. Never once considering that the events you expect might never happen."

He sucked in a breath.

She smiled. "Just kiss me. Let go. Let the future take care of itself."

He wanted nothing more than to kiss her and he knew what she was saying. He did always expect the worst. Except in his businesses—

What if that was the problem? He didn't fear his business life. That always worked out. His personal life scared him witless. Without all his mind-numbing work, he'd had a chance to have a personal life, but his brain couldn't handle it. It kept going back to his past, reminding him of his failures...

The answer seemed so obvious that he almost laughed.

Confusion disappeared and was replaced by hope, which seemed so simple...too simple. Yet people walked out on limbs every day.

Why couldn't he?

Why *shouldn't* he?

"Okay." She rose to her tiptoes. "Then I will kiss you."

The kiss was soft, soothing. He let her lead him until his breathing slowed and he couldn't think of anything but how much he liked her. He broke the kiss, pulled back, gazed into those soft eyes again.

She smiled at him. "Maybe the answer is to take things one step at a time. What if we pretended we just had tonight? What if everything didn't have to be serious?"

"Then I'd do this." He ran his fingers under the rim of her dress, where it stopped at the top of her arm. "And probably this," he said, gliding his hands to her hair. He luxuriated in the soft curls. Their gazes locked. The air crackled with possibility. But honesty sneaked up again and wouldn't let him play her game.

"I don't want to hurt you."

"I know." She shrugged daintily. "I've been hurt, remember? And I survived." She waited a beat. "Because you helped me to see that I needed to stand tall. Be strong. Now I am strong."

"You are."

"So, trust me. Trust us."

He lowered his head and kissed her like a starving man. Need poured through him, along with a sense he couldn't ever remember feeling. No pressure. No expectations. Just this minute.

He heard the sound of her bedroom door opening and pulled back. "Did you kick your door open?"

She laughed. "Yes, and backward."

"You are full of surprises." And hope and impossible joy mixed with common sense. When he didn't look forward, he couldn't look back. His mistakes didn't remind him of how easy it was to lose everything. He didn't see hurt or pain or the guilt that reflection always brought. He simply saw her.

She took his hand and led him into her room, then slapped his hands away when he reached to unbutton his shirt. Her nimble fingers worked the buttons, grazing his skin just enough to raise goose bumps and make him eager to be flesh against flesh with her. As she pulled his shirt from his trousers, he reached around and undid the zipper of her dress. One pass of his hands across her shoulders and the simple garment fell away, pooling at her feet.

He eased his hands under her hair and lifted it as he bent to kiss her. Silence and peace surrounded them.

And something more.

It wasn't the quiet contentment he'd felt before. He wouldn't call it serenity. It was more like normalcy…a sense of ordinary perfection that surrounded them like the glow of moonlight. As if he was exactly where he was supposed to be.

That fueled the fire of his need, but he refused to rush. With all the confusion in his life, his need to see and feel secure in his future, he never knew what it was like to feel normal. So, he went slowly, touched every inch of her soft skin, tortured her with teasing kisses and touches meant to send prickles of arousal through her.

He made love to her. Not in the childish, frenetic way he had with Skylar. Not in the sophisticated, practiced way he did with the women he dated. But as himself.

It almost did him in. As they soared to the heights and came back down again, he didn't know whether to laugh or weep. They nestled comfortably on the fat down pillows of her antique bed, and though sleep wanted to take him, for the first time in decades he fought it. He didn't want to miss a minute of "normal" with her. He lay quiet and content, waiting for his body to recharge in order to do it all again.

"So…" She hesitated. "Why don't you tell me about your wife?"

He laughed. With her nestled against him and his eyes closed, he suddenly understood the meaning of pillow talk. "Seriously? You want to discuss my ex after *that*?"

"If by 'that' you mean sex, then talking about your ex is tacky. If by 'that' you mean making love, then discussing your past is perfectly reasonable." She angled herself on her elbow. "Trace, you've done wonderful things for me. You gave me back my strength, my courage, my sense of self. And I've helped you too. But there's still something. Something deep that holds you back. Something that made me have to talk you into my room tonight... I want to hear."

He took a breath. With her on her elbow beside him, he didn't feel the weird sense that there was something he was supposed to be feeling or figuring out. His past was the past.

He turned until he could lay flat on his pillow, with one arm across his forehead. "The story doesn't paint me in a very good light."

Marcia lay down and snuggled against him again, realizing he might need some space to tell this part of his story. Not eye contact. "I don't care. I want to know."

He didn't say anything for a few seconds. Then he sighed. "Okay. You know how my friends call me Mr. Fix-It?"

She laughed. "After the way you handled my dad, I'd say the title's accurate."

"I think I've always had a little bit of that skill,

and before I found the right way to channel it, I used it for different things."

That puzzled her enough she levered herself to her elbow again so she could look down on him. "Different things?"

"To sweet-talk teachers into giving me extra time for projects or letting me do projects for extra credits, so I could obliterate the competition for valedictorian."

She laughed. "I can see you being a charmer."

"I was more than a charmer." He grimaced. "I don't want to say I manipulated people. But my talent seemed to go through phases before it found its true use."

She was glad he called his skill a talent and didn't think himself a bad kid because he'd gone after what he wanted. Still, putting everything together in her head, a not-quite-so-kind picture formed of how he saw himself. "You think you manipulated your ex-wife?"

"I wanted her. She was beautiful and smart and so damned fun to be around that I couldn't get enough of her." He drew in a long breath. "My family was good. But my dad had worries. I won't say he was a grouch, but he was a serious guy. My mom bustled about, trying to make everything perfect for him. My two sisters always had their noses in a book." He shrugged. "Skylar was free. She didn't worry. She had a place already secured in an Ivy League college. She didn't have to be concerned about grades or even SAT scores."

Marcia could picture it. A home where everyone was strung tight like a violin string and the introduction of a pretty girl who was the antithesis.

His voice softened. "She made me laugh. It was impossible not to love her. And I knew she was what I needed in my world."

"I think that's normal, Trace."

"Yes and no. I made elaborate plans to be around her. Being in the hall outside the door of her classes when she came out so I could walk her to her next class." He snorted. "I actually joined glee club."

She could picture that too and it made her laugh.

"But as direct as all that sounds, I like to think I wasn't obvious or obnoxious. We were friends before we became a couple and a couple for months before we became lovers."

She braced herself up again so she could study his face as he stared at the ceiling. "All still sounds normal."

"I guess the bad part starts when she got pregnant. Her parents were furious. Mine thought I'd ruined my bright future." He looked up at her. "I had scholarship offers. They thought I'd blown that."

"Had you?"

He winced. "After I talked Skylar into marrying

me, yeah. I had. Because her parents disowned her. I hadn't wanted them to support us, so I was sort of glad. It gave me a way to prove myself. And I did. With two part-time jobs, I made enough for us. But having two jobs and the responsibilities of a marriage and a baby, I didn't have time for school. We figured I'd go later, when things calmed down. But I lost the scholarships."

"Trace, all that is to be expected. I don't really see any manipulation."

"The manipulating happened when I talked her into marrying me. Her parents disowning her and me losing scholarships showed how badly I failed at trying to come up with a plan."

"You were eighteen."

"I talked her into doing things she didn't want to do."

"What things?"

He met her gaze. "She didn't want to get married. I talked her into it. Made promises." He waited a beat. His face shifted as he thought through what he would say next. "When Joshua died, all my promises meant nothing. She didn't have the same feelings for me that I had for her, so she bailed."

"That's on her."

"No! Don't you see? She never loved me. She loved the idea of doing the opposite of what her parents wanted her to do. I took advantage of that.

I gave her the path to rebel. And in the end, I got hurt."

"She's starting to sound like the bad guy here."

"Really? What if I hadn't provided the path for her to rebel? What if she'd had Joshua while living with her parents? What if they'd hired a nanny so she could stay in school? What if some-one had been there for Joshua the night—" He paused and swallowed, seemingly unable to get out the words *the night Joshua died*. Instead, he said, "*That* night?"

"Oh, Trace…" Her voice caught as the truth of what he was saying made her brain stumble. "You're blaming yourself for your son's death?"

He combed his fingers through his hair. "Sort of. I don't know. Possibilities always race through my head."

"Which is why you don't sleep."

He didn't say anything, just stared at the ceiling.

"You thought I was hard on myself?" She shook her head. "You are a hundred times worse to your-self."

She bent down and kissed him. Not for sex. Her heart burst with pain for him and the most basic kind of love: the connection of understand-ing combined with the longing to make him feel better.

The weirdest sensation trembled through Trace. He'd felt empty, cold, telling her his story, but as she kissed him, the cold dissolved in the face of her warmth. The emptiness edged away. Honesty opened a door. For the first time in his life he wasn't alone. She didn't have to say it. He didn't have to ask. They were partners.

He'd joked about it before, about them being partners in crime, but now he felt it.

He rolled her to her back and deepened the kiss. His past didn't melt away, didn't become irrelevant. He would carry the loss of his son forever, but he'd also carry the lessons learned from his mistakes, which made him a better man.

A man who might be able to commit again.

The thought tiptoed through his brain, and he savored it. Reveled in it. The emotion of making love became wild abandon and they rode the wave until they collapsed, exhausted, onto the softness of her bed.

What he felt for her went beyond what he'd ever felt with another person, and he had to wonder if this wasn't real love. Not just attraction. Not friendship. But a bonding of hearts and souls and purpose.

Purpose.

To run a vineyard together?

To marry and…

Have a family?

He might be coming to terms with his past, but the idea of having another child froze his limbs, stopped his heart.

He might forgive himself for losing Joshua. He might even see the potential for a future with Marcia. But he couldn't have another child, let alone enough children to fill the bedrooms of Giordano Vineyards' villa.

And Marcia would want children, a family. She loved family.

This was the thing that always stopped him in his tracks and caused his hesitation. *This* was what had made him really listen to her father's warnings about getting involved with her.

He couldn't give her what she wanted…what she needed. A family. He'd had his. And he'd blown it in the worst possible way. He absolutely would not have another child. He could go only so far with her before he began stealing away her dreams.

Stealing her dreams, the way he had stolen Skylar's.

That's why he shouldn't have let Marcia seduce him that night. Why he would stay away from her from now on. Loving Marcia when he couldn't give her what she wanted was as selfish, as wrong as talking Skylar into marrying him had been.

CHAPTER THIRTEEN

MARCIA SLID OUT of bed the next morning, letting Trace sleep. She showered, dressed and went to the kitchen, where she made a pot of coffee. Using her phone, she read her to-do list for the day.

When the kitchen doorknob rattled, her head jerked up and she saw her dad, trying to get in.

She walked over and opened the locked door. "Good morning, Papa."

He kissed her cheek. "Good morning. So where is Trace?"

She shrugged but grinned mischievously. "It's not my day to watch him."

He poured himself a cup of coffee. "Wherever he is, the three of us need to get together sometime today to talk about what you and Trace will need to have in place before the boys and I leave next week."

Her eyebrows rose. "Next week?"

"Yes." Mug of coffee in hand, he leaned against the kitchen counter. "I talked to Roberto and Mat-

teo and they have a few friends who can fill in for them while you hire others."

A bit taken aback but liking the idea of finally moving on to what she and Trace needed to do for Giordano Vineyards, she said, "That's good."

Fully dressed, Trace walked into the kitchen, "What's good?"

"Matteo and Roberto have friends who can fill in in the wine room."

Trace paused on his way to the coffeepot. "Oh, yeah?"

"Si." Antonio took a sip of coffee. "We need to be at White Gates next week."

He held Antonio's gaze. "Do you trust these friends?"

"Roberto and Matteo do. Plus, they are temps. People who can work for you while you find permanent replacements for Roberto and Matteo."

"And it's tourist season," Marcia put in, loving the way she and her dad had gone back to normal, all because of Trace's keen powers of observation. "But grape harvest is coming up. We have to be fully staffed by then."

Trace finished the walk to the coffee maker. "Sounds good."

Antonio nodded. "Sounds good."

Marcia smiled. The plan might be solid, but they also sounded like a team. Like coworkers who wanted what was best for everyone. Her heart expanded again. Everything was right in her world.

Her dad put his coffee cup in the sink and headed for the door. "It's almost time for the first bus."

Trace laughed. "I'll be out in a minute."

When her dad was gone, he poured himself a cup of coffee but stayed staring at the wall.

She walked up behind him and slid her arms around his waist, pressing her cheek to his back.

"I liked how much we sounded like a team."

He didn't turn around. "We always do."

He said it casually, but without emotion. After everything they'd shared the night before, she thought he'd be more open this morning. Still, what he'd told her after they'd made love hadn't been easy. It might take years for him to really be able to give himself to her, but she was patient. He deserved for her to be patient with him.

Later that afternoon, Trace sat behind his desk, putting the finishing touches on the plans for Giordano Vineyards. He'd made the necessary adjustments and now everything was set.

He could leave. Marcia could now run the vineyard alone. Yes, she'd have to hire staff, but Trace didn't need to be here to help her. She'd run this business with her dad for years. And with his one-year and five-year plans written for her to follow, he could be on the next plane back to Manhattan.

The thought froze him because he had nothing to go back to. But after the connection he and Marcia had made the night before, he knew they had fallen in love. He also knew that he could not have another child. Could not be a dad again. Which meant he could not give her a normal marriage. He couldn't give her children to fill Giordano Villa, the chaotic noise of her own family. Being around a child, even his own child, would be too painful. There'd be too many reminders of his lost son. He'd wear the guilt like a cloak, and that would cheat any kids he had with Marcia.

It was a vicious cycle.

Which was why leaving was the right thing to do.

He was just about to ask Marcia to come into his office, but he decided to make a call first. He casually rose and closed his office door, then called Wyatt and Cade from his laptop.

Wyatt said, "What's up?"

Trace laughed. "What do you mean what's up? Can't I just call to chat?"

Cade laughed. "No. You don't do things like that. Did you call to invite us to visit?"

Trace winced. "No, I still don't have furniture. Plus, I'm about to make arrangements to fly back to Manhattan this afternoon."

Wyatt sat up. "What?"

"There's not as much work here at the vineyard as I'd anticipated. Plus, Marcia's an experienced general manager." He shrugged. "It's been like a long vacation, but I'm ready to come home." He took a breath. "Actually, I'm ready to come back to work."

Cade quietly said, "You are?"

"Yeah." Trace said it eagerly, brightly, like buying a new business would be an adventure.

Wyatt cleared his throat. "Actually, we've already started something."

Trace frowned. "Without me?"

"Don't get your panties in a twist," Wyatt said. "We intended to call you once we had all the ducks in a row."

Cade sat taller. "I found a little manufacturing company that's undervalued."

"And once he found that," Wyatt said, "we focused our search and we found two other, similar businesses that we could buy and group together with the first one."

"They're all small," Cade continued, picking up where Wyatt left off. "We'll get only the one cheap."

"Yeah, we'll be paying full price for the other two," Wyatt agreed. "But it doesn't matter. The minute we group them, the value rises. We go in, clean up production, figure out a strategy that uses all three companies, and edge our way up the ladder in the market."

Trace's senses perked up. "These are manufacturing plants?"

Cade said, "Yes."

"What do they make?"

"A few things. We'll be bidding on government contracts."

He thought of Marcia, thought of leaving her, then reminded himself that she was better off without him. She'd find a man who wanted kids, fill the villa and have the kind of life she wanted.

"We haven't put in any bids or made any moves to buy them. If you think we're idiots, we can back off," Wyatt said with a laugh.

"But it does feel right," Cade said, his voice filled with temptation.

Trace's thoughts about Marcia faded away as his brain fully focused on the new businesses. Exactly what he wanted…what he *needed*. Not even twenty minutes to regret his decision to leave Giordano Vineyards, no time to change his mind and lots and lots of work to fill his brain. "How much money are we talking?"

"That's just it. If the three of us go together to buy these three companies, we don't even dent what we got for the sale of Three Guys Holding Company."

"It's like your vineyard," Wyatt said. "You paid only a drop of what we made from Three Guys and now that turkey will become a cash machine for you."

He didn't like the idea of thinking of Giordano Vineyards as being a cash cow. It was a home first and foremost...exactly why he had to leave. It couldn't be a home again until he gave Marcia the freedom to make it a home.

"I say we do it."

Cade laughed. "Really? We thought you'd tell us to take a hike."

"No. We're businessmen, not people of leisure. It's time to get back to work."

And now he was committed. No way to change his mind about leaving. After disconnecting the call, he searched for a flight out but couldn't get a seat until the next day. But that was okay—he could pack and be gone by noon.

Trace stayed in the wine room the rest of the afternoon and evening. When he entered the house, he turned and went to the master suite.

Marcia knew he wanted to shower, but he didn't come downstairs again. When waiting seemed foolish, she walked to her room. For a second, she debated going to *his* room, but something stopped her. He was absolutely a man of moods. Giving him space had worked so far. Like always she'd let him think this through.

The next morning, she found him at the desk in the office behind hers.

"Good morning."

He glanced up with a smile. "Good morning. Could you come in here, please?"

"Sure." Taking her coffee cup with her, she ambled into his office and sat on one of the chairs in front of his desk. "What's up?"

"I called my friends yesterday."

She gasped happily. "To invite them to visit?"

He folded his hands on his desk in front of him. "No. Basically, I was going to talk to them about looking for another investment. Turns out they'd already been looking. They've found a few businesses they want to buy to create a new company."

His answer was so unexpected, she blinked. "What?"

He chuckled. "I know! A ton of work. Reorganization. New corporation papers." He shook his head. "I see months of seven-day weeks ahead of us."

It took a second before she fully understood what he was saying. "You are leaving?"

"Yes. I have a flight out this afternoon."

Her heart stopped. "This afternoon?"

"Marcia, you are perfectly capable of running Giordano Vineyards. Your brothers can help you find the new employees we need. Your dad is good on his own—"

"Oh, so your work here is done?"

Clearly not happy with her interruption, he said, "Yes and no. I'll be back."

"When?"

"I'd say six months."

She gaped at him. "Six months!"

"Just for a review. Not to take over. You're

going to be fine. You ran this vineyard for your dad. You know—"

"Stop! Just stop acting like this is a work issue for me. I can run this place in my sleep...and without you. You're avoiding or ignoring the fact that there was something between us."

He pulled in a breath. "Maybe avoiding. But not ignoring. Yesterday, I came face-to-face with the fact that we needed to decide if you and I were headed somewhere or not."

"I thought we'd realized that thinking too much didn't work."

"The choice of spending a night together is very different than the making a choice that affects your whole life."

"And, obviously, you made the decision."

"I can't give you what you want."

"Oh, and what do I want?"

"Kids. A happy marriage." He shook his head. "I can't give you that."

"I didn't ask you to."

"No. But without even thinking too hard, I realized that if we kept going the way we were, no promises, no worries, years could go by. Years you would waste with a man who will never change his mind."

"You don't know that."

"Actually, I do."

Pain sliced through her chest like a knife. The impossibility of his actions rattled through her until she wondered why she was surprised. He'd never been able to take those final steps, to say he loved her...

Hell, for all she knew, he'd talked himself out of loving her.

There had always been something between them. Not quite a wall. Not as common as a barrier. A missing link.

"Do you really want to be with someone who is this much work? Always having to worry about my feelings, my past?"

Her eyes filled with tears, but she stopped them. "I never thought of you as work."

He rose from his seat. "Loving me has to be work, Marcia. I'm moody and demanding."

"You're also sweet and kind."

He shook his head. "More moody and demanding." He caught her gaze. "You deserve better."

She pushed herself out of her chair, forced herself to think like the smart woman she was. "I do deserve better." Though right at this moment that wasn't the issue. She'd pushed him the night before, tried to show him the way back to a good life. And he'd followed her, but this morning he'd had second thoughts.

She suddenly saw what he was saying. She wanted to be loved for real. Forever. He was telling her he couldn't do that. If she accepted that, she accepted less than what she wanted.

He walked around the desk. "I can see in your

eyes that you agree." Stopping in front of her, he lifted her face with one finger under her chin and said, "You make me forget. You make me happy. But part of me knows I don't deserve to be happy and that's the part that will always hold back. You deserve so much better."

She pulled away. The thudding of her heart in her chest slowed to a crawl. Her limbs felt like lead. She'd known all this, figured it out bit by bit, but had thought her love would be enough to keep him, to bring him back to life.

She might not be a chump this time, but once again she'd totally misread a situation.

He bent to retrieve a briefcase from beneath his desk, then stopped beside her again. "Fill the house with kids. Make the vineyard a home again. Enjoy this life."

Her lips trembled. "It's your life."

"I had thought it might be. Until I met you and realized it belonged to you."

"With you?"

He shook his head. "No. If I stay, I'll only hurt you." He bent and placed a gentle kiss on her mouth. Then he turned and left.

Her tears spilled over. Part of her begged her to run after him, to convince him to stay. The bruised and battered part simply couldn't do it. Adam had stolen from her family and made her a laughingstock. Trace had given her back her dignity. If she raced out, she'd lose it again.

As the reality of him leaving sank in, pain assaulted her and she realized her pride didn't matter. Then she heard the sound of her dad's old truck chugging into the parking lot and from the window watched Trace toss his things inside. And just that quickly he was gone.

Pain ripped through her. The tears that had been silently falling became gut-wrenching sobs. She raced out of the wine building through the back door and into the kitchen and found a note on the center island.

"I know how you felt about the Maserati. It's yours. Love, Trace."

She crumpled the note into a ball and would have tossed it into the trash, but she remembered the word *love* and swallowed hard. He had loved her after all.

But she hadn't been able to love him enough to heal the wounds that might forever haunt him.

She could not heal him. He could only heal himself.

CHAPTER FOURTEEN

TRACE DEPLANED AND had a car waiting to take him straight to Manhattan to the new offices Cade and Wyatt had rented. There'd be no furniture, but he was growing accustomed to empty or nearly empty rooms. Plus, he had a laptop. He could work anywhere.

And he needed to work. The flight from Italy to the United States had been long and lonely. With so much time on his hands to think, he'd about driven himself crazy.

Marcia's sadness had burned through him. Especially the pain that vibrated through her voice. Pain he had inflicted. The only comfort he had was knowing he would have ruined her life if he'd stayed. What wife wanted a husband who could never be happy? What woman wanted a man whose needs would always come before hers?

There wasn't a question in his mind that he'd done the right thing.

Using a private code, he rode the elevator of

the new building to the fiftieth floor and got off to the sounds of silence.

He leaned out and tried to see down the long hall. "Hello!"

No one answered.

Knowing Wyatt and Cade were supposed to be there, he called again. "Hello?"

"Back here."

That answer had come from Wyatt, but Cade appeared from behind the half wall in the empty reception area.

His voice a rushed whisper, he said, "Dude, I'm glad I caught you."

Trace laughed. "Really? Whispers? Are we keeping secrets from each other now?"

Cade made a frantic motion for Trace to lower his voice. "In the last forty-eight hours, we've talked to you, rented this space, put offers in on three companies and discovered Wyatt has a daughter."

Trace's eyes bulged. "What?"

Cade made the lower-your-voice motion again. "You need to be happy for him."

Confused, Trace whispered, "I do?"

"He was gobsmacked. Long story short, last year's girlfriend never told him she was pregnant."

"Okay—"

"What are you two doing out here?" Wyatt walked up the hall carrying a baby girl. He looked from Cade to Trace. "Gossiping?"

Cade shook his head. "No. No. We were just saying hello."

"So, you weren't telling him how my ex sprang a baby on me and bolted?"

Trace's eyes wanted to bulge again, but somehow, they hooked on the tiny girl dressed in pink. Scruffy hair told Trace Wyatt had probably been the one taking care of her overnight.

Jealousy roared through him. Until his loss, he'd always wanted a family. Wanted the responsibilities and the joys—

As quickly as he thought that, Joshua sprang to his mind. He'd had his chance and failed.

Pushing all that out of his mind, he walked over. "She's cute."

Wyatt said, "Looks like her mom."

"Where is her mom?"

Wyatt blew out his breath. "I don't know. Uganda. United Kingdom. United Arab Emirates. All I got was a heavy *U* sound, as she was shoving the kid into my arms and draping me with diaper bags."

Trace could picture it, and if suddenly becoming guardian for a child hadn't been so serious, he would have had to swallow back a laugh.

"DNA tests have already been arranged. But I have this feeling—a weird sense—that she's mine." Wyatt shoved the little girl into Trace's arms. "Here, hold her. While I get the papers you have to sign."

Having no choice but to take the baby, Trace settled her across his arm, the football hold he'd been taught when Joshua was first born. The baby smiled at him and his heart tumbled.

Good God. She was beautiful. So small and soft.

She gurgled a greeting and he laughed. "Hey, little one."

Wyatt stopped in his trip down the hall and turned to face him again. "Her name is Darcy."

"Darcy." He glanced down at the baby. Yearning wove through him. Memories of being a dad popped into his brain. The joy. The fulfillment. A love that surpassed anything he'd known. "Hey, Darcy."

As he spoke, her scent wafted up to him. The special combination of baby soaps and powders. Joshua had smelled like that. He'd loved his bath. And Trace didn't have to think at all to recall his blue eyes. His round face with chubby cheeks and tiny lips.

This time when his heart tumbled, it was painfully. He'd had a child, had a family, and he'd lost them.

He'd lost them.

Wyatt reappeared, stacks of papers in his hand. "I'll take her."

He glanced at Wyatt. His limbs had frozen. The baby powder scent filled the air now. If he closed his eyes, he could see his apartment with Skylar. Hear Joshua's laugh.

When he didn't move, Wyatt took his baby from his arms and handed him three packets of papers before he led him and Cade to three big offices at the end of the hall.

"I see why you chose this building, this space," he said, trying to be light and friendly, but the cruel memories of his son, his other life, haunted him.

"Everything's equal," Cade said, picking up the conversation as Wyatt guided them into the office with no desk, three folding chairs and a play yard filled with baby toys that sat beside a swing.

Wyatt slid the little girl into the padded seat of the swing.

Trace saw Joshua in a swing very similar to that one, laughing, as he talked to him while he made dinner and Skylar sat on the sofa reading a magazine. For the first time, the memories made him angry. And not at himself. Not even at Skylar. At the injustice of it.

He blinked away the images, forced himself into the conversations about the formal offers Wyatt had written for two of the companies and forgot about his son, his ex-wife, the life he'd tried to create.

But it lingered, haunted him, every time he looked at Darcy.

A week later, he stood by the wall of windows behind his brand-new desk, working to erase even one of the memories. His view of Manhattan stole his breath. He loved that it appeared as if he could reach out and touch the buildings around him, even though some of them were blocks away. But every time he saw Darcy, he saw Joshua. He remembered Skylar's snippiness, actually heard the discontent in her voice and wondered why the hell he hadn't seen it while it was happening.

"What are you doing?"

Trace spun away from the window to see Wyatt in his doorway. "I was looking at the…" He glanced at his desk. "Forecast for Green Peas and Ham." He sighed. "I still think that's a stupid name for a company."

"Then you should be coherent and vote when we have our meetings. Besides, we're going with the initials GP&H. No one needs to know what it stands for." He plopped on the seat in front of Trace's desk. "And by the way, I didn't buy that you'd been reading the forecast. You were staring out the window."

Trace shook his head, returned to his seat. Hands folded on his desk, he said, "Happy now?"

"No! I like you sharp with eagle eyes that find problems. I don't like this guy who came back from Italy with a broken heart. You said you were the one to end it with Marcia, so why are you moping around like a sad puppy?"

He tossed his glasses to his desk, then ran his hands down his face. "I'm not a sad puppy."

"Oh, please."

Darcy let out a shout and Wyatt sprang from his seat. "Be right back."

Seconds later, he returned with his daughter. Today she wore pajamas the color of a pumpkin. Something Wyatt had found online because he didn't like the clothes her mother had given him for her.

"I thought you hired a nanny."

"I did too. But something about her wasn't quite right."

Trace sighed.

"What? You don't like having the baby around?"

Part of him did. Part of him loved watching her, hearing her tiny voice. But every time he saw her, he thought of Marcia, then Joshua, and it was killing him. "She's no trouble... Now."

"Oh, I get it. She's no trouble now, but she will be when we hire employees."

"You know if you pawn her off on an assistant, someone hired to do accounting or write strategic plans, that woman's going to have grounds for a lawsuit."

"What if I ask a guy to watch her?"

Trace frowned. "I don't know."

"See? That's it right there. That's the problem. The old Trace would have known."

"Are you telling me I've gone soft?"

"I'm telling you something's wrong."

While orange-pajamaed Darcy crawled up her dad's chest, Trace tapped a pencil on his desk. His children with Marcia would have had black hair and his blue eyes. "I'm fine."

"You better be. We have a lot on the line here."

Right on cue, thoughts of Joshua drowned out his thoughts of Marcia, of their babies. Reminding him that life wasn't simple. Wasn't something he could conjure because he wanted it.

The next week, he tried to be sharper. He made spreadsheets. He created complicated to-do lists and made lists that reminded him of things. He swore to himself that nothing would get by him. He'd been present and helpful when they hired a receptionist and three assistants to handle the easy prep work. But twice Cade had to snap his fingers in front of Trace's nose when they were having a planning meeting.

Carrying Darcy, who wore blue jeans and a T-shirt that morning, Wyatt said, "Maybe you need to read up on government contracts some more."

"Okay. Yeah. I'll do that." He turned to go out of the room, embarrassed that he was slipping so much, but Darcy caught his eye. She gurgled and laughed.

His heart rolled into a ball, then expanded again.

Wyatt's shrewd eyes narrowed. "You know, if

it bugs you or distracts you that Darcy is here, maybe you should work from your penthouse."

His breath stuttered. "I'm not that bad." But every time he looked at Darcy, he saw the potential kids he could have with Marcia, the family. Then he'd think of Joshua and the vision would fade, kicked to the curb by the reminder that he hadn't been a good dad.

"You *are* that bad. It's been weeks since your return from Italy, and you're the saddest person I've ever seen."

Exhausted, about at the end of his rope, he took a seat on the chair in front of Wyatt's desk. He, Cade and Wyatt had never had a secret, and his current feelings suddenly felt like one. Especially since it was clearly affecting his work.

He took a breath. "Okay. I'll come clean. Every time I see Darcy, I think of Marcia."

Wyatt's eyes sharpened. "You see yourself having kids with her?"

"I don't know. Maybe. But it doesn't matter. As soon as I get the warm, fuzzy, oh-my-God-I-want-that feeling, I remember Joshua and the feeling turns to horror."

"Or fear."

Trace frowned. "Whatever."

Wyatt sighed. "Don't you think it's natural that you'd be afraid to start another family?"

Trace shrugged. "Sure. I guess. I don't know."

"Hey. Don't shrug that off! When you had too

much time on your hands, you thought about your family. So, to get rid of that, you bought a business thousands of miles away so you could forget again. But you didn't forget. You found a woman, fell in love, and all your old longings came back—and you remembered your son. So, you ran again."

"I'm not running from having another family."

"No. You're running to stop the memories of losing a child." Wyatt glanced down at Darcy. "Honestly, Trace, I can't imagine the pain." He looked up and caught Trace's gaze. "And for you, I'd probably toss in a sense of failure. But twelve years have passed. You're not a kid anymore. And you're back to wanting the dream."

Trace swallowed. "Dreams don't always turn out the way we want."

Wyatt laughed, bouncing Darcy when her lips puckered and she looked like she might cry. "Don't I know it." Wyatt shook his head. "This is life," he said, angling his chin down at his baby. "Surprises. Pains. Wins and losses. You can't run from it. You can't hide. And you sure as hell shouldn't be blaming yourself for something that wasn't your fault."

When Wyatt seemed so sure, Trace groaned. "How do you know it wasn't my fault?"

"Because I know you. You make lists. You go over plans a million times looking for flaws. You do more than your share of the work and then some. Trace, you didn't fail. Something went wrong with the worst possible results. But it wasn't your fault."

Trace said nothing. He felt frozen. Tired. Tired of running.

"Go to Italy. Tell that woman you love her."

Everything Wyatt had said fluttered through him. With his defenses down, new questions filled his brain.

What if he hadn't been at fault? He wasn't so foolish that he didn't realize that some things really were out of a person's control. Even if that person was a nitpicky, detail-oriented brainiac.

Still, he was tired of going over it in his head, looking for a mistake.

Maybe it really was time to let go?

To try again.

With Marcia.

Time to let himself be himself. He would never forget his son, but he couldn't stop living. Or he'd lose Marcia to another man, and unless he got rid of Giordano Vineyards, he'd watch her fall in love, marry and have kids with someone else. While he sat at a desk, buried in work because he was afraid to try.

Marcia kept herself busy hiring staff. Her dad talked nonstop about what a great guy Trace was, but her mother was wise enough to see Marcia wasn't interested and she constantly changed the subject.

At nights, she'd sit by the pool, missing Trace, going over almost every word they'd said, trying to find a way to bring him back to her, but nothing stuck out. He'd told her about losing his child. He'd given her details about his ex. He could have talked forever about Cade and Wyatt. But he couldn't tell her he loved her.

Except in a note. And then only as a sign-off. A throwaway word.

She supposed she understood. His commitment to his business partners was just that. Business. His sorrow over his son and the loss of his marriage... Those might be the past, but he'd loved the life he'd set up for himself, and she genuinely believed he wanted it back.

In a weird kind of way, she realized he didn't want a future. He wanted his past back.

It was nuts to want something he couldn't have... But maybe that was the point. He didn't want a future filled with twists and turns and surprises. He wanted his past fixed. Or maybe a future he could control.

Once or twice she slept on the chaise by the pool instead of her room, but after two weeks, she'd compartmentalized her feelings for him and worked to be her old self again. When her mother invited her to have lunch with her in the village, she hesitated, but knew it was time to move on.

With everything.

They entered the tavern, their eyes adjusting to

the lack of light, and Mama told the hostess there would be just two of them.

When they were seated, Gina raced over with her order pad, a silly smile lighting her face.

"Hello, Gina," her mother said, her normal sweet self.

"Hello, Mrs. Giordano."

"How have you been?"

"I'm great." She held out her hand, showing off an engagement ring. "Look."

Marcia's mother gasped. "That's beautiful! Congratulations!"

Marcia looked at the ring too. Her heart tugged and she thought of Trace, but she shoved those memories out of her head. "It's lovely. Your fiancé has great taste."

"It's not as fancy as the ring you got from that guy… What was his name? Adam? But at least we know my guy will stick around."

Marcia smiled. Funny how the mention of Adam barely registered. He was so far in her past that her heart didn't even tweak. "That's true."

"Rumor has it you ran off Giordano Vineyards' new owner too." She leaned in and added, "There was gossip you were sleeping together, but I stopped it."

Marcia counted to ten. Did this woman never let up?

Her mother pressed her lips together.

"I told people there were plenty of reasons the

two of you were living together. That it might not be about sex."

This time Marcia heard the baiting in Gina's voice, so she only smiled.

"Besides, it's not like every man in the world is smitten with you," Gina said on a laugh.

Finally done with this, the gossip, the speculation, the out-and-out stupidity of caring what this woman thought, Marcia shook her head. "You know what, Gina? You need to get out more. If the only thing you can think about is my love life, you have got to be really bored." She smiled thinly. "Go to a museum. Take a ride somewhere out of town. Broaden your horizons."

Gina gave her a puzzled look before she took their drink orders. When she scampered away, Marcia's mother laughed.

"That was interesting."

Marcia rolled her eyes. "No. It wasn't. I've heard something from her every damned time I've come into this tavern since Adam left me. Today, I just got tired of it and turned it back on her."

Her mother patted her hand. "And you did it so nicely I'm not even sure she knows what hit her." She patted her hand again. "That's the Marcia I love."

"Really?"

"Yes. Now I think what you need to do is go to Manhattan and tell that Trace a few things."

This time Marcia laughed. "I pushed him as

hard as I could push when he told me he was leaving. Deep down, Trace is a wonderful guy. He lost a marriage and a child when he was young. He will never get over them."

"But he loved you. I could see it in his eyes."

She shook her head. "Doesn't matter."

She said it simply, easily, but her mother frowned. "Of course it matters. Just like getting the last word with Gina mattered. Marcia, you cannot let everyone walk all over you just because you made one mistake. You need to go to Manhattan."

"And do what?"

"Tell him you're not letting him leave you. Tell him he needs to come back to Italy."

"He can't. He and his partners have new projects now. New businesses they are buying."

A shaft of light from the front door opening skimmed over their table, then retreated as the door closed.

"Plus, I'm not begging a man to stay."

"You wouldn't be begging. You'd be putting your foot down."

Marcia laughed, but stopped suddenly when she saw Trace out of the corner of her eye. Within seconds he was at her table. The chatty, noisy bar silenced.

"Hey."

She looked up at him. "Hey." He looked great. A little thinner, but his face was different. Not tight. His eyes weren't shrewd or calculating. His face looked—

Relaxed?

"Can I sit?"

Mama quickly shifted to the seat next to hers so Trace could have the chair beside Marcia. "Sure."

"Did you come back for grape harvest?"

His eyes widened. "Oh, my gosh! Is that this week?"

"My dad is thinking Saturday."

"I…" He laughed. "You know what? Yeah. I want to be here for grape harvest."

Marcia worked up a smile. "Great."

"But first, there's something we need to talk about." His eyes shifted to her mother, then back to her.

Mama said, "I think I'll go to the ladies' room," and was gone within seconds.

Marcia noticed the whole bar seemed to be watching them and she groaned internally.

"What is it about the vineyard that concerns you?"

He took a breath. "It isn't the vineyard. It's about me…well, us. I made a big mistake…or maybe not really a mistake. I saw a future for us, and every time I did, I would think of my son and make the assumption that I couldn't have other kids because I'd always think of him when I saw them."

"I believe we talked about something like that the last night we slept together."

"Yeah. But it didn't hit home enough. I knew that every time I'd think about the future, thoughts of Joshua would drown it out. Making me feel I had no options but work. But it took seeing Darcy—Wyatt's baby daughter—to make me think of Joshua—"

"I'm so sorry."

He sniffed. "Don't be. At first she brought back awful memories. Then she made me want a baby so much I couldn't even be around her. She smelled like him. She even looked a little like him and I just kept longing for another chance."

"She broke you."

"Her and a talk with Wyatt. It was like seeing her every day pushed me past that point of fear that always rose up when I'd think about having another child...with you."

She said nothing. Her heart filled with sadness for him, but she also saw what he was saying.

"Did you ever stop to think that maybe your longing for a child started after you sold your business? That time on your hands didn't have you thinking about your past. It had you thinking about your future..."

"Yes. I figured that out once I got back to Manhattan. In fact, I think that was the thing that was bugging me. The thing that didn't fit. I hadn't thought of my past in a decade. I thought it had popped up because I had too much time on my hands. But what actually happened was time on my hands had me thinking about a future. When I did, the past came back to haunt me. Making me think I couldn't have a future."

"So you're good?"

He smiled. "Very good. Good enough to be able to say that I want to spend the rest of my life with you. To have kids running around all over the vineyard. But most of all, to just watch it all and do it all *with you*." He pulled a jeweler's box from his jacket pocket, lifted the lid and exposed a diamond the likes of which Marcia had never seen before. Her gaze leaped to his.

"Will you marry me?"

Her breath stuttered. Her heart expanded with joy. "Oh, my God."

Silence stretched between them.

The bartender shouted, "Answer already!"

A general rumble of laughter rode through the tavern.

Tears filled her eyes. "It seems everyone is on your side."

His eyes filled with humor. "Oh, I'll bet half of them are hoping you say no. If only for the gossip."

She laughed but said, "That means the other half is hoping I'll say yes."

He took the ring from the box. "If you add me in, that tips the scales."

She held out her hand. "Wouldn't want to ruin your equation."

The ring hovered over her finger. "You need to say the words."

She blinked back tears and said, "Yes. I will marry you."

When he slid the ring on her finger, they both rose and she threw herself into his arms. "I never thought you'd come back."

He rained kisses on her face. "Wyatt's baby wasn't the only thing that made me sad. Every time I saw her, I thought of you..."

She pulled back. "So, you missed me?"

"Every damn second of every damned day."

She laughed through her tears. "I missed you too."

"Let's go home."

From behind her, Mama said, "Leave the Maserati and I'll be fine."

She laughed. Trace laughed. "Should we leave her the car? I have a rental."

"Yes. Let's leave her the car."

Trace tossed his set of keys to her. "No scratches or dings."

Mama caught them. "I'm not promising anything."

They left the bar amid shouts of congratulations, and when they stepped outside, the sunlight burned their eyes.

"This would have been so much more romantic at night...under the moon."

She stood on her tiptoes and kissed him. "I couldn't have waited that long."

He slid his hands around her waist. "I couldn't have either." He paused a beat. Then he looked into her eyes. "I am so sorry I left you."

She grinned. "I'm not. It might have been a few long weeks, but if that's what it took for you to work it all out, then it was worth it."

He kissed her long and deep, happiness singing through his soul. "Oh, it was definitely worth it."

EPILOGUE

THE FOLLOWING SPRING, on White Gates Vineyards, Trace stood at a makeshift altar, waiting for his bride. The place had been spruced up, and Antonio and his sons were making progress toward getting the winemaking up and running again. Deciding to be married on her parents' vineyard had been a way to honor them, and Trace had taken it.

With Wyatt and Cade at his side, he watched the arch decorated with white roses, waiting for Marcia and her dad. Her friend Janine, serving as bridesmaid, appeared first. Smiling, glad to be with Marcia after months of mourning her mom, she looked elegant in her pale blue gown.

Then Marcia and her dad stepped under the arch and his breath stuttered. After her myriad shopping trips when she accompanied him when he was needed in Manhattan, he'd expected her to wear something bold and outrageous. Instead she wore an old-fashioned lace dress and an airy tulle veil that billowed in the breeze.

The ceremony was quick, and his eyes had misted as they said their vows. He would never hurt her. She would never hurt him. Not because they were perfect but because each understood real love. Each knew *trust* was a verb.

They also wanted the same things, came to this relationship as mature adults, ready to face the future together.

They posed for pictures for over an hour, then ate an early dinner under white tents decorated with roses. Wine flowed freely. Everyone danced late into the night. His parents and sisters had become close with Marcia's parents and brothers, and though Trace suspected a little hanky-panky between the Jackson sisters and the Giordano brothers, he said nothing. From here on out, he let nature take its course. He didn't brood. He didn't overplan. He let himself be himself.

When they could finally leave, he carried Marcia to the Maserati. Because the top was down, he dumped her in the passenger's seat without opening the door, and she laughed.

"Is this how I can expect you'll be treating me now that we're married?"

He hopped into the car, caught her hand and kissed it. "Oh, I expect to treat you very well tonight."

Her laughter rang out as they roared down the lane of White Gates and headed for their home.

Their home.

A real home.

A combination of his parents' common sense and the Giordano love of life, it would be a very happy home indeed.

* * * * *

*Look out for the next story in
the A Billion-Dollar Family trilogy*

Coming soon!

*And if you enjoyed this story,
check out these other great reads from
Susan Meier*

**Stolen Kiss with Her Billionaire Boss
Hired by the Unexpected Billionaire
The Bodyguard and the Heiress**

All available now!